VENGEANCE VALLEY

Vengeance Valley

GEORGE G. GILMAN

NEW ENGLISH LIBRARY
TIMES MIRROR

For:
J.G.
a small cog in the Edge wheel but relatively important.

A New English Library Original
© 1975 George G. Gilman

*

FIRST NEL PAPERBACK EDITION NOVEMBER 1975

*

NEL Books are published by
New English Library Limited from Barnard's Inn, Holborn, London, E.C.1.
Made and printed in Great Britain by Hunt Barnard Printing Ltd., Aylesbury, Bucks.

45002488 1

Chapter One

THE man at a second storey window of the Lone Star Saloon breathed in deeply of the warm, late morning air and looked down on the main street of Greenville. The street was like the room at his back in one respect – neat and clean. Then he raised his eyes to make a raking survey over the broad valley: his vantage point high on the western slope of the long depression in the land of south-west Texas. It, too, was neat and clean. All of it in keeping with the man who owned the valley, the town, and everything in the valley and town. Except the man at the second storey window: for nobody owned Edge. Not even Woodrow Ryan.

The verdant valley and the neat town were quiet beneath the peaceful sky in which there was not a single cloud. And for a full five minutes Edge stood at the window, contemplating what might have been: thinking about a farm on the prairie of Iowa and another farm beside a lake in the Dakotas. At no time did he consider what still might be for this was no longer his way. The lessons of the past had been too hard and too painful. Fate had decreed that this man had no right to plan – or even hope – for the future: not if such plans or hopes demanded an absence of violence and death. For, if he claimed such a right, the result was as inevitable as night following day – his capacity to endure mental anguish would once more be put to the test. And he was not sure just how low his resources in this respect had fallen. So he lived for the day, the hour or even the minute: content to survive and confident of his ability to do this, no matter what degree of physical suffering was involved.

A gentle breeze was breathing warmly from the southern end of the valley and on it was carried the appetising aromas of many meals in the process of cooking. The smells broke his train of thought and he turned from the window and crossed the room to the bureau with a mirror fitted into its high back. There was a bowl of cold water on the bureau, with a bar of soap and a razor alongside it. He stripped off his red under-shirt and started to wash up and shave off a thirty-six-hour growth of bristles.

He had to stoop to see the reflection of his face in the mirror, for he was a very tall man. Six feet three inches without his boots on. The mirrored image showed a long, lean face with piercing blue eyes looking out from under deeply cut brows. Beneath the eyes, his cheek-bones were high, flanking the start of the steep slope of his hawklike nose. His mouth was wide and narrow lipped above a firm, strong jawline. The skin of the face was stretched taut over the bone structure, burnished to a dark brown by heritage and exposure to every kind of weather: and deeply scored, particularly around the mouth and at the corners of the eyes, by both age and long experience of depri-vation and suffering. Age was the lesser responsibility, for the man was only in his mid-thirties. The frame of the face was the long, thick, dark black hair that reached down to brush his shoulders and the base of his neck. It was the face of a man with mixed blood coursing through his veins: some of the features inherited from a Mexican father and others passed on by a Scandinavian mother.

The body beneath the face was deceptively lean, for the man weighed a solid two hundred pounds and carried not an ounce of excess fat. On his chest was a thick matting of hair, as black as that on his head. The firm flesh, which had the texture of well-used leather, was olive-brown in colour, except for the white scar tissue of an old bullet wound on his left shoulder. There were other areas of scarring on him – at the nape of his neck, beneath his hair, and on his right hip and left thigh con-cealed by his long johns. Three of the wounds inflicted by Rebel soldiers during the War Between the States and the furrow across the nape of his neck acting as a constant reminder – if such was needed – of how close he had come to death since the end of that conflict.

Washed and shaved, he started to dress. Riding boots, pants, shirt and hat. All travel-stained but still serviceable. The single holster gunbelt had the same qualities. He spun the cylinder of the Army Model Colt before sliding it into the tied down holster. Then he checked the action of the Winchester after picking it up from the floor beside the rumpled bed. Finally, he wiped the steel blade of the wooden handled open razor and eased the implement, become a weapon, into the leather pouch that hung on a beaded thong at the back of his neck. His hair concealed the top of the handle and it would take a keen eye to read anything dangerous into the faint, elongated hump where his shirt contoured the sheathed razor.

As he let himself out of the room and went along the landing and down the stairway, it would require more than a mere passing glance to spot the even subtler signs that the man called Edge was a man to be wary of.

'Afternoon, sir!' the young, bespectacled man behind the desk in the lobby greeted brightly. 'It certainly is a fine day, isn't it?'

The city suited desk clerk was too bright – making too much of an effort at being friendly. It was a fake mood to front his nervousness and he was not making a very good job of it. The atmosphere in the shabby lobby was pleasantly cool, yet the clerk's wan face became sheened with sweat in the time it took Edge to move from the foot of the stairs to the desk.

'Do somethin' for you, sir?' The clerk's lower lip quivered and there was a tremor in his voice. He did not look into the ice-blue eyes of the tall half-breed who towered almost a foot higher than him. But he had already given his guest more than a passing glance. Yesterday Edge and an old lady had entered the Lone Star, a gun covering two of Woodrow Ryan's meanest hands. In one of the upstairs rooms, with Mr Ryan as a witness, two people had died. A guest and the old lady. Edge had not been responsible for either sudden death. Not to the extent of squeezing a trigger, anyway. But the clerk, who considered himself a well-schooled student of human nature, attached moral blame to the tall stranger. As Edge had checked in following the double shooting, the clerk had looked long and hard, if surreptitiously, at the new guest.

The clear blue eyes were the major clue. They looked incapable of smiling. Then there was the mouth. The thin lips did fold back to reveal even, very white teeth but the humour of the expression never spread beyond the extent of the skin creases from the corners of the mouth. And, in repose, the mouth adopted a line that was either bitter or cruel. Then there was the way the man carried himself. He was a quiet, loose-limbed mover: apparently incapable of haste. But this, too, was a façade. Behind it, he was constantly poised to spring into instant action should his ever-alert eyes detect a hint of danger.

Added to all this was Edge's total lack of emotion following the explosion of violence.

This man, the clerk decided, was no stranger to danger and death for he was himself both dangerous and deadly. Hardly a man at all, except in basic appearance. Under this outer shell he had the mind and reflexes of some kind of animal: a beast of prey who was himself preyed upon by others. And such a man, the clerk considered, would possess a quick temper. Thus, the clerk went to great lengths to avoid antagonising Edge.

'Like to pay what I owe and check out,' the half-breed replied evenly, aware of the reason for the clerk's nervousness. Everywhere he went, men of perception were able to detect the aura of death that emanated from him. But he believed he could not help what he had become: and considered there was no point in either excusing or defending what he was.

'Leaving Greenville, sir?' The clerk used a red and white spotted kerchief to mop the beads of sweat from his forehead.

Edge showed the clerk his mouth-only smile that made the blue strips of his narrowed eyes colder than ever. 'The Lone Star's got a rooms-for-rent monopoly in this town and I don't plan to sleep on the sidewalk, feller.'

The clerk tried a smile of his own and succeeded in looking a little sick. 'It's just that Mr Ryan will be in later today, sir. And he did say he wanted to talk to you.'

'How much for the room?' Edge asked, sliding his bankroll from a hip pocket. It was a large wad of bills. Twenty-five hundred dollars for completing the job that brought him to Greenville, plus the stake he had carried with him before he tied up with the ill-fated women he did the work for.

'Ten dollars, sir. That includes livery of your horse, sir.'

Edge nodded and counted off the money. 'You run a good hotel, feller. So I reckon my horse did all right, too.'

'Mr Ryan demands the best of everything, sir.' The clerk

hurriedly wrote out a receipt for the room rent. The attempt at a smile had been abandoned and the pale young face was set in grim lines as the receipt changed hands. 'He also likes people to do like he says, sir.'

Edge slid the receipt into his pocket with the bankroll and canted the Winchester to his shoulder. 'If I happen to run into him, I'll tell him you're doing a good job here, feller.'

He turned and ambled over to the door.

'I'd be obliged if you'll tell him I gave you the message!' the clerk called. 'Mr Ryan really doesn't like it at all when people don't do what he tells them.'

'I get the message, feller,' the half-breed answered without turning around as he pushed out through the door.

His eyes closed to even narrower slits as he stepped into the bright, Texas sunlight. The aroma of cooking food was stronger than ever now and the street was not so quiet as before. The stores and other places of business were closing up for lunch and people were moving along the sidewalks towards their neat homes or the Rio Grande Restaurant a block and a half south of the hotel. And a few men were riding in on horseback and buckboards from the crop fields and pastures in the immediate vicinity of Greenville. Dust from under lazily moving hooves and slowly turning wheels rose into the heated air and floated back down to the street again.

Moving down to the restaurant, Edge saw the grey motes settling on to his clothes and felt them against the skin of his face, held there by the sweat which had started to ooze the moment he came out of the shade. And he sensed many pairs of eyes watching him. It was obvious that, while he had slept, the story of the violence which marked his arrival in town had been told and retold. But there was no resentment in the stares directed towards him as he made his easy progress down the street. And none of the observers got close enough to him to experience the kind of nervousness in his presence which had gripped the desk clerk. As the object of the surveillance, Edge sensed simply an expectant curiosity.

When he reached the doorway of the restaurant, he shot an easy glance back up the street towards the front of the Lone Star Saloon. The desk clerk was standing between the two rocking chairs flanking the entrance, his glasses removed in order to focus his gaze across a block and a half. He seemed agitated at being discovered watching Edge, and he snapped his head around and began to talk fast to a young boy sitting astride a pony. The boy nodded forcefully, accepted something small and glittering from the clerk, and heeled his mount into a fast gallop. He rode out of the north end of town, onto the trail that curved down the valley slope.

Edge pushed open the door and stepped into the restaurant. For a moment, a dozen conversations continued to make a pleasant buzzing sound in the cool interior. Then, as the people spread among the tables turned their attention towards the new customer, talk faltered and stopped. The half-breed could smile with genuine humour when the occasion demanded it, and he did so now, sweeping his blue-eyed gaze over the expectant faces.

It was the only smile in the room, which wasn't unusual for Greenville. The clerk's pathetic attempt to hide his attack of nerves was the closest thing Edge had seen to happiness since he rode into town more than twenty-four hours ago. Neatness, cleanliness and peace did not breed contentment in Woodrow Ryan's town and valley.

He took off his hat and hooked it over a stand just inside the door. 'Sure hope the food in this place matches the smell and not the faces of you folks,' he said evenly, starting to weave between the gingham-covered tables to a vacant place in a rear corner.

'Mr Ryan demands the best of everything,' a woman answered, as all eyes followed the half-breed.

Edge dropped into a chair that put his back to the corner, and leaned his Winchester against the wall. The woman was middle-aged and fat. She sat on a stool behind a short length of counter and her enormous breasts were flopped and spread on the counter top. Her dress was the same chequered pattern as the tablecloths. Her straw-coloured hair was drawn back severely off her fleshy, over-painted face. Thus, her grimly insulted expression was blatantly plain to see.

'Should have remembered, ma'am,' Edge told her. 'Feller down at the hotel already said that.'

'Includin' the best table,' the fat woman went on. 'Which you're sittin' at.'

Edge glanced around him again, then down at the table

immediately in front of him. All the other tables, in use or vacant, were laid with steel knives, forks and spoons, paper napkins and glass condiment sets. The one he had chosen was arrayed in engraved silver and linen.

'Ryan expected?'

'We never know if he's expected until he's here. But even if he don't come, he won't like to know somebody else has sat at his table.'

'What the hell, Lizzie?' a man sitting with three others growled. 'You give him the warnin'. Stranger wants to sit there, let him.'

'It's all right for you, Nathan!' the fat Lizzie countered. 'Won't be you moppin' the blood off the floor if Mr Ryan or one of his men comes in here.'

She returned her glare to Edge.

He sighed. 'There's no blood when a man dies of hunger, ma'am,' he said wryly.

Lizzie gave a sigh of her own, which sent ripples all the way to the curved crests of her large breasts. Then she flashed a toothy smile that emphasised every one of her considerable number of wrinkles. 'Serve the gent, Greta!' she yelled over her shoulder, then returned her attention to Edge. 'Can't no one say you weren't given the warnin', mister. And, seein' as how you're settin' yourself up for trouble, I sure hope you get it.' She suddenly spoke more quickly. 'And I ain't wishin' nothin' bad for you, mister. Just for whoever tangles with you.'

'And I reckon that goes for everyone in here!' a man agreed enthusiastically. He wore a white smock with scissors and a comb showing at the breast pocket.

'Ain't no doubt about that, not no way,' another man put in. 'I surely am achin' to see a Ryan man taken down a peg or two. And this feller sure looks the kind could do it.'

'He don't only look the kind,' a woman customer contributed excitedly. 'I was out on the street yesterday. Saw the way he handled Hardin' and Carver.'

Edge wasn't listening to the flattering comments being spoken about him. Greta – a skinny, short-haired girl of about twenty with bad skin and a lisp – had given him a menu and he was choosing his lunch. By the time he had ordered, the Rio Grande was buzzing with conversations again. Now there was an almost tangible atmosphere of subdued excitement in the restaurant and the glances directed towards the half-breed had become surreptitious again. The expressions in the eyes were a mixture of admiration and rueful pity.

But, as time slid by – Edge eating soup, a steak and trimmings, then apple pie – the tension subsided. Some of the customers even left to start their afternoon chores, their disappointment at the non-appearance of Ryan or any of his men plain to see. Then, just as Edge was about to start on his end of meal coffee, the message sent out by the hotel desk clerk produced a reaction. Galloping hoofbeats sounded against the sun-baked surface of the street and the gentle breeze from the south tossed little billows of dust in through the open windows of the restaurant.

Lizzie and the dozen or so customers remaining in the Rio Grande suddenly looked as if they no longer relished the prospect of witnessing rare trouble from such close quarters. Four riders skidded their mounts to a noisy halt outside. The barber attempted to leave, but backed off hurriedly from the opening door.

Edge lifted the coffee cup to his lips and eyed the quartet of newcomers over the tilted rim. He recognised Harding and Carver from yesterday. Both in their mid-twenties, broadly-built and hard-eyed, they were the two men Edge had been forced to get by in order to reach Woodrow Ryan at the Lone Star Hotel. From the way they halted on the threshold and glared at the half-breed, they were still smarting from the ignominy of that minor humiliation. Behind them were two older men. One about forty and the other five years younger. The forty-year-old was only an inch or so above five feet in height, but he was the broadest and heaviest of the lot: his shirt and pants contouring flesh that looked as if it was as hard as granite. His bare arms and square-cut face certainly had the visual texture of rock stained dark brown. His hat hung down his back to show close-cropped, iron-grey hair. He had green eyes with bloodshot surrounds. The fourth man was a slighter, thinner, slightly shorter variation on the tough pattern of Harding and Carver. All the men were sheened by sweat and their clothing was filmed by the dust of a long, hard ride.

'That's him, Harv!' the blond Harding said breathlessly, jerking a black gloved hand towards Edge.

'An' the snot-nose is sittin' at Mr Ryan's special table!' the dark-eyed Carver exclaimed, his tone incredulous. He switched his gaze towards the fat woman. 'What the hell, Lizzie?'

The big breasts trembled. 'I told him,' she excused. 'Ain't one customer in here can say I didn't tell him.' She swallowed hard and glanced briefly at Edge. 'But he ain't the kind of feller I want to get into a hassle with.'

The short, wide Harv stepped between Harding and Carver and draped a hand over his holstered Remington. His eyes, their green the colour of the scum on a stagnant pool, remained locked on the impassive gaze of the half-breed. 'On your feet, drifter!' he snapped. 'And wait at another table.'

Edge lowered his cup slowly on to the saucer. 'You're confused after the ride in the sun, feller,' he said easily. 'I'm the customer. Greta's the one who waits at table.'

Harv was a fast draw specialist. He yanked the Remington from the holster, cocked and levelled it in a continuous smooth action. 'No one gets funny with the foreman of the Big R spread!' he snarled.

The Remington was aimed between several tables at Edge. The people at those tables were poised to dive for safety, but none of them moved. Harding, Carver and the other travel-stained man cupped the butts of their sixguns but did not draw.

The half-breed nodded and dug a hand into his shirt pocket for the makings. 'Seems to me it's a serious business living in this part of the country.'

'Move, or I plug you!' Harv ordered. His voice was as brittle as spring ice.

Edge sprinkled tobacco in a paper, spread it and then licked the paper and rolled the cigarette. 'Make it a good shot, feller,' he invited. He hung the cigarette at the corner of his mouth and reached over his shoulder to strike a match on the wall. Then he lit the cigarette and his eyes were suddenly staring with increased power through the cloud of blue smoke. His voice was no louder, but its tone matched the stare. 'Ryan likes the best of everything.'

For a stretched second, Harv went on the boil and might have squeezed the trigger of the Remington. The tension building behind the half-breed's casual exterior might have been strong enough to spring him clear of the bullet. But then the might have beens were immaterial. Harv was not aware he had been bluffing until Edge called him. Then he realised his predicament, the naming of his boss driving home the point.

Edge gave the man time to think of something, removing the cigarette and sipping at his coffee.

'Harv . . .'

'Shuddup, George!' the foreman snapped, and abruptly holstered his gun – slower, but just as smooth as the draw had been. Then a sneer altered the lines of his face. 'Okay, drifter! You called it right. Mr Ryan wants to talk to you and a dead man won't give him no answers.'

'You oughta plugged him someplace that wouldn't kill him, Harv,' George said with disappointment.

'Shuddup!' Harv growled, and pointed to a vacant table just inside the door. 'Lizzie, fetch four mugs of Java here.'

He sat down first, and the others followed with reluctance. The fat woman yelled the coffee order over her shoulder. The barber scuttled out of the Rio Grande. Greta delivered the coffees and gradually the other customers summoned enough courage to rise from their tables and run the gauntlet of the scowling Ryan men to pass through the door. They all paid their checks to Lizzie, who eyed them with envy for the way they could escape the tense atmosphere of the restaurant.

Edge finished his coffee and cigarette at the same time and approached the counter behind which the fat woman sat. The men at the table near the door stiffened when the half-breed picked up the leaning Winchester. They were only a little less rigid after he had canted it casually to his shoulder.

'Be two dollars,' Lizzie said, a little hoarsely.

'Tasted as good as it smelled, ma'am,' Edge told her as he handed over the money. 'If I'm ever through this town again, I'll –'

'You ain't through Greenville the first time yet, drifter!' Harv cut in coldly.

Chair legs scraped and footfalls thudded as Edge slowly turned away from the counter. The Big R foreman remained on his chair. Harding, Carver and George had aligned themselves across the doorway. Hands hovered close to guns, but didn't touch them. The expressions on the faces of the standing men were grimly intent. Only Harv looked a little anxious and it was obviously a mood he did not experience often.

The half-breed sighed. 'I have this thing about being on the wrong end of a gun, feller,' he told Harv evenly. 'Now you aimed your Remington at me without knowing about it. Every man ought to be allowed one mistake.' He nodded towards the standing men. 'Any of those fellers draw, be like you made two mistakes. On account of you're the foreman and they're just hands. So best they shoot to kill and let Ryan whistle for answers. Best for you, feller. Unless you'd rather be dead than mess up the chore Ryan gave you.'

Anxiety became full-fledged fear for a moment, before Harv could tighten his mouthline and stop his lower lip trembling. Across the width of the sunlit restaurant, the foreman spotted the quality which the clerk at the hotel had seen at close quarters. But Harv had good reason to be afraid. He was not only facing a killer. He was in a situation where the possibility of sudden death was hovering in the hot air.

'Look!' he suddenly roared, electing to use blustering anger as a shield for his true feelings. 'Why the hassle, drifter? Mr Ryan wants to talk to you, is all. I happen to know what about. He's got a job in mind for you. And he ain't no skinflint when it comes to paying his hands.' He moderated his tone and his discomfiture increased. 'He'll be comin' into town later today. When he got word you was plannin' to leave, he sent us in to keep you here.' Harv shrugged and spread his hands, palms open and fingers splayed. 'Me and the boys will be happy to spend the time anywhere. Here, in your hotel room . . . ' He grinned suddenly. 'Or maybe in the barroom of the Lone Star. Hot day like it is, that's a pretty good place to spend . . . '

Edge moved away from the counter, weaving between the tables to reach the door. 'What kind of job?' he cut in.

'Kind one of us could do!' Carver growled. He made as if to spit, but stopped himself.

'Shuddup!' Harv commanded, and returned his attention to Edge. Easy money job, Edge. Couple of land surveyors are down here from San Francisco. Gonna make a map of the Big R spread. They need a guard and Mr Ryan reckons you're the man to ride along with the big city soft types.'

The half-breed halted six feet in front of the trio of men barring his exit.

'Course, I don't know what Mr Ryan plans to pay you!' Harv hurried on. 'But it won't be no chickenfeed, I can tell you that.'

'Tell these fellers something,' Edge invited.

'What?'

'To move out of my way.'

'Snot-nose!' Carver snarled.

'High-handed bastard!' Harding added.

George shot an excited glance at the Big R foreman. 'Say the word, Harv!' he urged.

'Okay!' Harv yelled. 'I . . . no!'

Angry, then terrified. The trio in the doorway went for their sixguns between the speaking of the first word and the last. None of them was as fast as Harv had shown himself to be. The fat Lizzie had time to scream and fall backwards off her stool to gain the cover of the counter. And the half-breed was able to get his ticket out of the Rio Grande Restaurant. He whirled in front of the drawing guns, the rifle still canted to his right shoulder. Then he folded forward fast from the waist, left hand streaking to the back of his neck. Coffee cups scattered from under his chest and belly and were smashed on the floor. Harv's anger had gone and the terror had replaced it. The short and wide foreman tried to push back his chair and rise from the table. His chair hit the wall beside the doorway as the three men swung to bring their drawn guns on to target. Harv started to power upright, both hands hooked over the lip of the table. Edge flicked his right wrist as his left hand streaked away from the back of his neck.

The Winchester swung forward and its barrel suddenly formed a bar across the crook of Harv's neck on his left side. The gleaming blade of the razor was a less weighty pressure against the other side of the man's pumping throat. The two men were in an eyeball to eyeball confrontation, the hawkish nose of Edge and the snub nose of the foreman almost touching. The half-breed's back, stretched across the disarrayed table, was totally exposed to the levelled Colts of the three men crowding the doorway.

'Harv!' George yelled. 'We can take him!'

For perhaps two seconds the only sounds in the restaurant were the fast breathing of Lizzie in hiding and the drip of coffee from the corner of a tablecloth onto the floor. A trickle of saliva oozed from the mouth of Harv and coursed down his chin. His green eyes – suddenly wide – now looked as wet as stagnant pools.

Edge's voice was as cold as his ice-blue eyes. 'No one to

talk to and no foreman. Be a lousy day for a feller who likes the best of everything.' His thin lips folded back to show the merest hint of a mirthless smile. 'But that won't be our problem, Harv.'

'He's already given us the word!' Carver snarled, turning slightly to give himself an even clearer shot at Edge.

'No!' Harv croaked, his eyes screwing in their sockets, down and to the right. Vision confirmed what the twitching nerves at the side of his throat had told him. He was within a split-second of being slashed open from ear to ear. His words ran into each other, and more saliva was spilled. 'I didn't mean that, you trigger-happy lunkheads. I said okay for the drifter to leave. I was gonna say move outta his way.'

There was another short interlude of near silence.

'Gee, Harv, what now?' George exclaimed.

'Better pick your words real careful this time,' Edge encouraged softly.

The foreman, still frozen into his half standing, half seated posture, swallowed hard. The in and out movement of his flesh caused the razor to dig into the skin. A single droplet of blood squeezed from the cut and mingled with the sweat beads coursing down his neck and under his shirt collar.

'You tell 'em what you want!' Harv croaked.

'Ain't much with words,' the half-breed replied. 'Man of action, I guess. How about some from them.'

'What?' Harv said.

'Toss their guns over to the far side of the room. Then they go down the street to the hotel livery and get my horse. Black and white stallion. Ought to look well-fed and groomed for the price I got charged.'

The foreman managed to tear his gaze away from Edge's level, unblinking stare. The dull green eyes swivelled to the far left of the sockets this time, to focus on the Big R hands.

'Do like the drifter wants!' he rasped.

'But Harv . . . ?' George groaned. He swung his head to look imploringly at Harding and Carver. 'We can take him before . . . '

Anger almost surfaced through the expression of fear. It came across stronger in the foreman's voice. 'Do it, you crazy bastard! All of you. It ain't a shave this guy's fixin' to give me.'

'Just a close one at the moment,' Edge put in softly.

'Mr Ryan won't like seein' Rhoda in black!' Harv yelled, his voice pitching higher.

The brief silence this time was total. The coffee which had been spilled was now dry. Fat Lizzie was holding her wheezy breath. Edge did not take his eyes away from the sweat-sheened face of Harv. The muscles in his left hand became tauter, preparing to drag the blade of the razor deep and long across the leathery skin of Harv's throat. But there were no crashing shots and no feeling of lead tearing into the firm flesh of his back. Just an outward rush of air from the lungs of the three hands. Then the thumping of their sixguns as the weapons hit the floor in a far corner of the restaurant.

The foreman's breath was slower as it was expelled. Hot and foul smelling against the half-breed's face. The green eyes swivelled to meet the blue ones again. 'I'm Mr Ryan's brother-in-law,' he said to explain the 'lady in black' comment that had clinched the backdown.

'And seems like the drifter's king of the friggin' law around here,' Harding snarled.

'My kingdom – and his life – for a horse,' Edge answered.

'Go get his damn nag!' Harv ordered.

Having surrendered, the trio of hands realised the futility of further delay. As they whirled and tramped out of the restaurant, Lizzie climbed back onto her stool.

'Mr Ryan ain't gonna like this at all,' the fat woman said.

'What the hell are you people lookin' at?' Carver yelled out on the street. 'Get back to your friggin' own business.'

'Ease out the Remington slow, feller,' Edge instructed. 'Drop it on the floor, then stand up.'

'What you gonna do?' Harv asked, and his tongue darted out to keep more saliva from spilling. He had lost a lot of body water through his mouth and pores.

'You first.'

The foreman followed the order. When his gun had clunked to the floor, the pressure of the Winchester barrel was relieved. The half-breed straightened at the same rate as his prisoner. The honed blade of the razor never left its resting place against the congealed blood of the tiny cut. Not even when Edge put the Winchester on the table and moved around to tower head and shoulders above Harv.

'This is crazy!' the foreman said, his arms held rigidly at his sides as the backs of his knees pressed against his chair. 'To talk about a job is all Mr Ryan wanted.'

Edge hooked a foot around the Remington and scaled the gun across the floor. 'Should have asked polite, feller. And I'd have give you my answer polite. I don't want a job.'

'You shouldn't have sat at Mr Ryan's table!' Harv countered, some of his fear ebbing.

'Wanted to see me,' Edge answered. 'Seemed like a good place to meet up around lunch time. Now I know what he wanted to see me about, I ain't interested.'

The foreman's confidence was mounting by the moment. The blade was still against his flesh but there was no longer tension in the hot air of the restaurant. 'Then you better ride fast and long, drifter. For twenty miles in any direction from Greenville, it's Big R land. Folks who don't live on the spread or folks that don't do what Mr Ryan wants . . . well, they ain't nothin' but trespassers. And Mr Ryan don't take kindly to trespassers.'

'Obliged for the warning, feller,' the half-breed said as he heard the sound of a horse being led slowly along the street. 'Kind of repays that one I gave you about guns being pointed at me.'

There was no change in Edge's impassive expression and no alteration in his level tones. But suddenly tension flooded back into the atmosphere. Harv was abruptly as rigid as a rock. Lizzie caught her breath.

'The boys mistook my meaning!' the foreman croaked, his voice bursting from his throat and blowing wide his compressed lips.

'One mistake is all, feller,' Edge replied. 'I told you that.'

His left hand moved in a blur of speed. Harv tried to move backwards. The chair blocked him and he sat down hard, a cry of alarm venting from his gaping mouth. Edge's left hand, fisted around the razor, rose from the foreman's neck to his temple. It went down to maintain its threat as Harv was forced to sit. Then it whipped down lower to deliver on the threat.

The point of the razor sank into the thin covering of flesh beside the green eye until it hit bone. Then the slash across the cheek took the honed steel deeper into more meaty flesh with no solid support beneath it. The tip of the metal penetrated into the inside of the mouth for half an inch. Then the half-breed started the withdrawal, jerking the crimson stained blade clear just before it would have torn through the corner of Harv's mouth.

As Edge stepped back, scooping up the Winchester, the blood started to show. It was like a vividly coloured curtain as it oozed from the slashed flesh and crept down over the lower half of the injured man's cheek. He didn't scream. The sound that emerged from his mouth as he slumped in the chair was a loud moan. The blood that bubbled over his lower lip was flecked with the white of saliva.

'My God, mister!' Lizzie gasped, gathering her weighty breasts in her arms and hugging herself as she stared in horror at the terrible wound. 'What kind of a man are you to do somethin' like that?'

Edge halted in the doorway and eyed her without emotion as he put on his hat. 'I can be any sort, ma'am, depending on how I'm treated.' He wiped the razor on the already stained table-cloth and slid it back into the neck sheath.

'But he was okay just now,' Lizzie insisted. 'Gave you a warnin' he didn't have to.'

'So I treated him okay,' the half-breed said with the trace of a smile. 'Polite even. Didn't cut him dead.'

As Edge went out through the door into the sunlight, Harv started to moan again, as he raised a hand to his cheek and stared at the crimson wetness on his palm. But the sounds he made were soft, as if he lacked the strength to put power behind them.

Out on the street, the black and white stallion was hitched to the rail immediately in front of the restaurant. Harding, Carver and George stood off to the side a little way. A little mad and a little embarrassed. They somehow looked partially undressed without guns in their holsters. There was nobody else on the street but, as Edge swung into the saddle, booted the Winchester, and leaned forward to untie the reins, he sensed many eyes keeping secret watch on him.

'What happens now?' George snarled while the other two merely stared with bitter hatred at the mounted half-breed.

'Don't know about the plans of you fellers, but I'm leaving,' Edge said, wheeling his horse gently to head him towards the south.

The injured man inside the Rio Grande Restaurant gave a

louder moan: just high enough to reach out into the sunlight.

'What happened to Harv London?' Harding demanded, staring at the open doorway and trying to penetrate the deep shade inside.

'Guess you could say his face come apart,' Edge called over his shoulder as he urged the stallion forward. 'Why don't you fellers locate the town doctor and go and join him.'

Chapter Two

THERE was a river – a tributary of the Rio Grande border marker between Texas and Mexico – that flowed slow and shallow down the entire length of Woodrow Ryan's valley. And it was on a bend of this river, where it cut from the west to the east and ran into an extensive stand of timber, that the tall half-breed made night camp.

He knew he was still on land claimed by the Big R for he had ridden at a measured, easy pace through the heat of the afternoon and the coolness of evening. Greenville was long out of sight behind the rolling green hills and rocky outcrops that featured the valley floor and gently sloping sides. He had angled off the main trail to El Paso soon after leaving town, to follow a series of loops and spurs that linked small farmsteads set amid the swathes of cornfields and spreads of pastureland. There were women and children doing the chores close to the houses. Men worked in the fields or rode herd on grazing cattle. Heads were raised and eyes watched him. But nobody ever called out a greeting and Edge never rode close enough to invite conversation.

Then, as twilight spread down over the valley in the wake of the setting sun, the worked land slid behind the lone rider astride the big stallion. And he entered the wild, undeveloped country. Immediately, the atmosphere changed, and he knew it had nothing to do with the coolness of the evening air after the heat of the day. Nor was it entirely because he was alone again – the way he liked to be. He did feel, and relish, the experience of once more being the ultimate loner: totally on his own, self-reliant and requiring nothing of nobody but himself.

But, as he gathered wood from the fringe of the timber stand, lit a fire, scooped water from the river and boiled it for coffee – he thought about why the sensation of being alone should be so intense and so gratifying.

It was unconnected with the break away from the Big R hands. Such incidents he took for granted. He either survived or he did not. If he survived, it was never with a sense of triumph. For, by decree of a cruel fate, he survived only to face a new danger from a new quarter. Perhaps from the same one in this case, for he had not covered more than three-quarters of the twenty mile trespass limit Harv London had spoken of.

It was one of the many lessons he had learned during the brutal and bitter fighting between the Union and the Confederacy. If a man indulged in the luxury of a false sense of security at the end of a successful battle, it could blunt his quality of alertness when the next bout of violence exploded.

Then, as he sipped at his first mug of coffee and smoked a cigarette, the pensive half-breed pinned down the reason for which he had been searching. It was the people of the town and the valley farmsteads he was glad to put behind him. Or, rather, the mood of the people which generated an atmosphere even more oppressive than the Texas heat. An atmosphere comprised of many emotions: all of them bad. Of fear, of sadness, of depression and of despair. But, most of all, perhaps, of disappointment.

As Edge drank his second cup of coffee and smoked another cigarette, his contentment was complete. Now that he knew what had been troubling him about Greenville and the valley, he was able to clear his mind. Because it was not his concern.

He looked up at the clear sky hung with a half moon and myriad stars and decided the night was not going to get cold enough to warrant a fire. So he added no kindling to the flames before stretching out on the soft turf of the river bank and drawing a blanket over his fully clad body. He lay with his right arm under the blanket, hand draped over the butt of the Army Colt. His left arm was outside, brown-fingered hand on the grass within an inch of the Winchester's brass frame. His hat was tipped forward over his face to shield his eyes from the bluish light of the moon and stars.

His mind, hovering on the blurred dividing line between waking and sleeping, played host to many memories. Of a town called Hate where fear was the main contributory factor to the tension that was wrapped around every citizen and every building. Another town called Rainbow where he had come closest to dying. Summer, where he met Elizabeth Day. Peaceville where Jamie's killers paid so highly for their crime. Seascape and a girl in a golden cage. Andersonville in the war. Richmond and Jefferson Davis. Oregon, the Dakotas, California, Mexico and Nevada. Places and people crowded in on Edge's mind. Places where the people or the Government paid him money to make trouble his concern. Just a few places where love for a brother and a different kind of love for a wife gave him a less venal and far more powerful motive to concern himself.

Then, as they always did, the images from the violent past retreated before the man's need for rest. And Edge slept, between the fire and the slow-moving river, behind a low hump two hundred yards from the fringe of trees. But it was no ordinary sleep. It never was, even when he was totally immune from danger. Experience of walking the thin dividing line that separated troubled life from sudden death had formed his sleeping as well as his waking habits. And at rest there was even more of the animal about Edge. For, while he relaxed and replenished the store of energy depleted by the day, a part of him remained strangely alert to what was happening around him. Some kind of sixth sense was awake and attuned to pick up the first hint of danger. And, once its warning was transmitted to the man's mind, his physical being was immediately roused and prepared for defence and retaliation.

A pebble rattled against a rock.

The half-breed's eyes snapped open against the solid darkness beneath his hat. He knew the sound had come from beyond the hump of ground – over towards the trees.

'Quiet, you damn fool!' a man rasped.

They were out of the trees. Less than fifty yards away. At least two of them.

'Yeah, watch it, Kelsey. This guy is likely to be real twitchy.'

At least three of them. Moving very quietly now, their foot-

falls not making a sound against the springy turf. Edge released
the butt of his Colt and drew his right arm out from under the
blanket. He slid his hat off his face. The moon had changed its
position a little. The fire was no more than a patch of grey and
black ashes with just a tiny glow of red here and there. Edge
guessed he had been sleeping about two hours. He drew in a
silent breath and raised the back of his head off the ground.
Nothing showed against the silvered river on his right. On his
left and beyond his splayed legs a broad arc of flat terrain was
empty. They had not started to circle him yet.

His left hand had closed around the frame of the Winchester
immediately he awoke. There was no need to pump the action
for the first shot. There was already a bullet in the breech and
the hammer was back. The breath was let out of his lungs as
silently as he had sucked it in. One of the men approaching
him was breathing with a lot more noise. Edge drew fresh
breath and powered himself into a roll. The blanket went with
him and was under his belly as he stopped the roll, elbows
stabbing into the turf, stock-plate against his shoulder and eye
behind the back-sight of the Winchester. The barrel of the
rifle was tilted over the crest of the hump, aimed down the
shallow fall off of land towards the timber.

The three men were less than sixty feet away, rooted to the
ground by the shock of the half-breed's sudden move. Edge
saw them only in silhouette, solid black against the slightly
lighter coloration of the trees behind them. But the attitude of
their frozen stance made it obvious they had rifles thrust out in
front of them.

The Winchester exploded three times in quick succession,
the shots separated by the minimum time it took a man to
pump the rifle's action. The men yelled with one voice at the
sound of the first shot. By the time the third report sounded
against the night, every rifle had been hurled to the ground
and every arm was flung high in the air. The three bullets had
crashed and thudded into the trees by then, after cracking
within an inch of the head of each man.

'Mister, we don't mean you no harm!' one of the men
shrieked.

'You ain't done me none yet,' Edge called in reply, pumping another shell into the breech. 'Convince me you're as honest
as you're noisy.'

The men looked at each other and their spokesman was tacitly elected.

'Can we come closer, mister? It's kinda hard to shout after the scare you give me.'

'Six feet's a good distance,' Edge allowed. 'Remind you how deep under you'll go if you can't soft talk me out of blasting you.'

The man chosen to do the talking led the way. But the other two were hard behind him, like kids afraid to be left alone in the dark country. If they wore gunbelts, they were hidden under the ankle-length, fully-buttoned topcoats the men wore. As they came closer, Edge stood up, stepped over the hump and then sat down on it. He rested the Winchester across his thighs and took out the makings. But his narrowed eyes, the moonlight reflected off them as though they were slivers of glass, never left the men. They called a halt themselves, double the distance away that Edge had specified. All of them were still reaching up towards the bright stars.

'This is mighty straining on shoulder muscles as old and overworked as ours, mister.'

'Your idea,' Edge reminded them, striking a match on the Winchester stock and lighting his cigarette.

'We can take 'em down?'

'It was the best idea you fellers had all night.'

'He means keep 'em up, Selby,' the man on the left said nervously.

'I know that, Yates!' Selby growled.

'So get the business done, Selby!' the third man urged. 'The quicker the better for my rheumatics.'

All the men were pushing hard towards sixty. Selby was a head taller than the other two but all had frames that looked as if they had been strong in earlier times. There was still strength of character in their burnished year-lined faces. But life had been harsh and, if they had not exactly given up, they were finding it hard to keep stoking their will power.

'We're farmers, mister,' Selby said, his slack lips moving more than the words demanded. But it wasn't fear anymore. Just old age and a reaction to the shock. 'Honest men.'

'A man's line of business earns him money,' Edge replied. 'Don't guarantee his word.'

'Tell him what we want, Selby,' Yates impressed wearily.

'We didn't come out here for no –'

'Heard about you from Luther Inman – barber over at Greenville.'

'He complain I do my own shaving?'

The third man managed a harsh laugh. 'Sure told us you made a lousy job of takin' the whiskers off Woodrow Ryan's brother-in-law.'

'Pack it in, Kelsey!' Yates snarled. 'Even if this guy ain't for pluggin' us, I reckon as how Ryan men are out huntin' him.'

'We wanna offer you a job, mister,' Selby said quickly.

Edge sighed. 'Seems the barber didn't tell you fellers everything. I made it plain I didn't want a job.'

Kelsey gave another laugh. 'Plain, he says. Harv London was made real ugly gettin' the message.'

Yates spat, took a step forward and lowered his arms. The half-breed's hands were already on the Winchester, leaving the cigarette slanting from the corner of his mouth. He didn't move the gun, but all three farmers were aware he could move it and blast them in three blinks of an eye.

'Look, Edge!' Yates rapped out. 'This valley was homestead country. Us three and a lot like us come here years ago and started to work the land. Then Woodrow Ryan moved in from the east. With a lot of money and as many men as it took. And papers, mister. Signed and sealed papers from the land office in El Paso that claimed he had title to the whole damn valley.'

'He's tellin' it like it is, mister!' Selby encouraged.

'And maybe he'll get it finished if he gets the chance,' the half-breed replied.

'Yeah, quiet Selby,' Kelsey augmented, deadly earnest now that the turkey talk had started.

'From being owners of our own land, we was suddenly his tenant farmers,' Yates went on, wiping spilled saliva from his grizzled jaw. 'And he made us an offer. Cut on everything we got off our land, or we got off our land.'

Edge nodded. 'Some farmers might be honest men,' he allowed. 'But ain't many of them got a head for business. If Ryan's got the papers, he's got legal title. I ain't no lawyer, so go find yourself one while I get back to sleep.'

The half-breed's advice, although the men had no intention

of taking it, encouraged Selby and Kelsey to lower their arms without fear.

Yates was shaking his head. 'We tried the law way back at the beginnin', mister. And it didn't do no good. On account of Ryan can afford to buy the law just the same as anythin' else he takes a fancy to.'

'But he couldn't buy you!' Selby put in.

'Nor scare you!' Kelsey added.

The half-breed showed a cold grin, but the moonlight striking his teeth gave off a refraction as icy as that from his eyes. 'I haven't been scared since I was five years old that I recall. And I only work when I need the money. Just like I sleep when I'm tired.'

'We reckon we can raise ten grand, Edge,' Yates said softly. 'Small job, be over in a few days. With ten grand you wouldn't have to work in a long time.'

He tried to make his tone persuasive. But all that came across was a note of pleading.

'Just to lead us is all,' Selby urged. 'You stood up to Ryan's men and you walked away. Ain't ever been anyone in the valley who ever did that.'

Kelsey cleared his throat and spat. 'Leastways, not since ten years ago. When Elric Fuller and his two sons stood up to the Ryan. Got carried away – to Greenville Cemetery.'

Yates waited impatiently for the slower speaking man to finish. Then he stared at Edge earnestly as the half-breed took the cigarette from his mouth and arced it out into the river. 'Everyone in the valley is gonna get the word about what you done, mister. And you're gonna be more popular than St Peter. If you stick around for awhile – and, like I said, it'll be worth it to you – folks'll rally. We'll have the numbers and the spirit to stand up to Ryan and his men.'

'Yeah!' Selby said excitedly, his eyes shining.

'We'll really show them bastards!' Kelsey added.

'Luck to you,' Edge offered.

'We don't need luck!' Yates snarled. 'We need you!'

'Don't talk bad to him,' Selby advised hurriedly.

Yates continued to glare for long moments, then his expression became one of pleading. He even extended both gnarled hands out in front of him in a begging gesture. 'Ten grand is gonna be hard enough to raise, mister. But, if it's a question of money, name your price.'

The half-breed shook his head. 'Ain't no more questions about anything, feller. Only ever was one. You asked it and I told you no. Be obliged now if you –'

'Hit the soil, Edge!' a familiar voice yelled.

It was followed by a series of other sounds. Voices raised to urge horses forward. Animal snorts. Splashing water. Battle cries that were like echoes from the war. Hoofbeats on grass. The cracking reports of rifle fire and the crackling of sixguns firing. By the time the initial burst of sound was over, the three farmers had whirled to stare at the point where the river ran into the trees. And the half-breed had spun in the sitting posture and tipped himself sideways off the hump.

He stayed down, pressed tight to the turf and protected by the hump, as lead began to sing through the air immediately above him, in counterpoint to the noise in the near distance. But he had seen the riders as he turned. A dozen of them, galloping out of the trees in a well-ordered line of advance, spread out from the river-bank across fifty yards of terrain. The first shots had been exploded into the night sky, from rifles and revolvers held high above the heads of the riders.

One man – at the centre of the line – was not firing. He rode without a weapon in his hand and it was his voice Edge had recognised. Woodrow Ryan.

As the men galloped closer, they angled their guns downwards. Bullets skimmed close to the three farmers without tearing into flesh: for the trio's screams continued to ring with terror rather than pain.

The battle cries ceased. Then the shooting. Voices called for a halt to the advance and the horses snorted into a slower pace and came to a stop. The screams of the farmers lost stridency and became sobs and groans of despair. Edge rose onto all fours and then pushed himself erect. His left hand was still wrapped around the brass frame of the Winchester. But he pointed the rifle negligently at the ground as he raked his narrow-eyed gaze over the faces of the mounted men.

The line of advance had curled in at the flanks as the riders neared their objective, so that now it was formed into a half circle with the farmers and Edge covered on three sides. Selby, Kelsey and Yates had taken the first few steps towards scattering when the attack opened. But then, as the hail of lead streaked around them, they halted and clawed their hands high again. They remained almost frozen in this posture now, shaking just a little as they fought to control their terror.

The mounted men looked down at those on the ground with expressions that ranged from bitter hatred to amused contempt. Woodrow Ryan switched between the two extremes as his gaze swept back and forth between the farmers and Edge.

The rancher was a big man in his middle years with slicked down, thinning grey hair and a neatly clipped, pointed beard of the same colour. A handsome man with powerful features dominated by dark, penetrating eyes. A suntanned man who looked fit and was well-fed and well-dressed. A man who emanated calm self-assurance and a belief in himself and everything he chose to do. A man who now held a double-barrelled shotgun crossways in front of his chest: looking as comfortable with it as if he had been born with it like that.

'Edge,' he said, his voice rich and mellow. 'That answer you just gave these homesteaders is about the most important thing you ever said in your life. Means you get to go on livin' it.'

'What life is all about,' the half-breed said softly. 'Living.'

'Mr Ryan!' Kelsey croaked.

A Winchester was tipped forward and fired. Kelsey yelled and jumped a full twelve inches into the air as the bullet thudded against the ground between his boots.

'You guys are through with talkin',' Carver growled, resting the stock-plate of his smoking rifle on his thigh.

He was on Ryan's right. Harding was on the rancher's left. George was among the men, too. Edge did not recognise the rest. Harv London was not there.

'What'd my horse do?' the half-breed asked.

The big stallion had reared once against its tether when the noise exploded. A few moments later the animal had been hit a dozen times. He lay now where he had crumpled and rolled, the blood no longer oozing from the head and side wounds.

'Got in the way of Big R guns,' Ryan replied simply. 'I breed the best animals west of the Mississippi and you'll get one to replace him. Later. Right now, I'll thank you to disarm yourself and step aside.'

Edge knew it wasn't going to be as easy as Ryan made it sound. If he was to be allowed to ride away from the river bank – and he trusted Ryan's word on this – it would not be without payment. And the rich rancher had no need of further money. But the half-breed could do nothing except resign himself to what was to happen. There was an alternative, but it was suicidal. So he allowed the Winchester to drop from his loosened grip. He followed it with his gunbelt.

'The blade, snot-nose!' Carver ordered, sneering in triumph as he levelled his rifle.

Edge eased the razor from the neck pouch and let it fall onto the discarded gunbelt.

Harding vented a harsh laugh as he joined Carver in training a rifle on the tall, impassive-faced half-breed. 'Guess you got that bad feelin' again, drifter? Being on the wrong end of guns.'

Edge nodded. 'You know the score, feller.'

'We sure do!' George called gleefully. 'Twelve to four.'

'Ain't the final innings yet.'

'Step aside, Edge,' Ryan repeated, and moved his shotgun. He aimed it at Yates who was at the centre of the short line of farmers.'

'Please?' Selby cried.

Yates looked over his shoulder at Edge as the half-breed moved out of the line of fire from the shotgun. With the inevitable set to happen, Yates managed to inject controlled bitterness into his tone. 'Thanks for nothin',' he rasped. 'They got the weapons off you easy as takin' playthin's off a baby.'

Edge showed a cold grin as he stopped and turned beyond the margin of safety from shotgun blast. 'They got such a disarming way about them,' he muttered.

Ryan squeezed one of the triggers: and Yates died before he could swing his head and see his killer again. The range was ten feet and the charge took him in the centre of the chest, with the outer fringes of the pattern hitting the face, arms and belly. Yates, blood spraying from his limp body and pieces of flesh dropping away from him, was lifted and hurled several feet across the turf. Even before his shattered corpse hit the ground, Selby had turned to run and Kelsey had dropped to his knees and clasped his shaking hands together.

'Mr Ryan, I beg of you!' Kelsey pleaded.

Only the title and name were heard. The second barrel of the shotgun exploded its awesome noise to drown the rest of the entreaty. The lumbering Selby was hit in the back of the neck and his body smacked to the ground a full two seconds before his severed head. That was hurled several feet farther to drop into the ashes of Edge's fire. Dust rose from under it as the flood of escaping blood hissed and sizzled, dousing the remaining embers.

'It's not happenin', it's not happenin',' Kelsey screamed, toppling forward and clawing at the grass with hands become talons.

Ryan, eyes as empty as those of the two dead men, stared at the prostrated man and reloaded his smoking gun by feel. Both barrels. Kelsey had crawled three feet towards his executioner when the shotgun was locked together and aimed down at him. Kelsey raised his head to transmit a final, tacit plea. His mouth worked frantically but the only sound to emerge was something between a gurgle and a choke. He stared down the double black holes of the gun muzzles, then pushed his face into the grass and clamped his hands over his head.

The first barrel belched shot, smoke and noise. The hands, arms and head of Kelsey disintegrated in a great splash of crimson flecked with white. The gun was elevated a fraction and exploded again. An enormous red hole appeared in the lower back of the already dead man. Soggy red flesh scattered across the rich, dark green grass.

Ryan raised the shotgun to slant it across the front of his broad, expensively garbed chest again. But one handed this time. The barrels were too hot to hold.

'You keep bad company, Edge,' the rancher said evenly, with just the trace of a rebuke behind the words.

The half-breed raked unemotional eyes over the remains of the farmers. Selby's torso and head; Kelsey's body with the gaping hole in the back and a head and parts of his limbs reduced to scattered pulp; and Yates who had a bubbled red pool where once his chest had been.

'Two's company, feller,' he said, matching Ryan's tone. 'And you sure turned three into a crowd.'

Chapter Three

ONLY Woodrow Ryan remained mounted after his nod had signalled the others to slide from their saddles. All the rifles were back in the boots and it was just sixguns which were aimed at the half-breed as the dismounted men encircled and closed in on him.

'I'm a hard man, Edge,' the big rancher said, taking out a ready-filled pipe and clamping it between his teeth. He continued to speak, around the stem. 'A man don't get to be what I am with what I got by bein' soft. But I claim also to be a fair man.'

Edge nodded. 'Guess there was a chance that scatter gun could've blown up in your hands and made a hash of you instead of them,' he allowed wryly.

Ryan made a dismissive gesture with his free hand. 'Those men abused the fair shake I gave them. Let them keep workin' on my spread and make enough to take care of themselves and their families. But I heard every word of that proposition they put to you. Dogs that bite the hand that feeds them deserve what them three got.'

'Some put down,' Edge said softly as the two biggest of Ryan's men moved in to flank him, holstering their guns.

Both were at least two inches taller than the half-breed and there was nothing lean about their frames or faces. They were taller and even broader versions of Harv London and, like the Big R foreman, neither of them carried any padding of fat. The two handed grips they fastened around Edge's upper arms and wrists felt like iron claws as they locked into position.

'Forget about them, Edge,' Ryan went on after he had lit his pipe and the aromatic smoke was covering the acrid taint of exploded powder. 'Their problems are over. A man like you has many still to face.'

Harding and Carver stood in front of Edge, guns in their holsters and grins of anticipation on their faces. Three men were aligned on either side, also with guns back in the leather. But eager hands draped butts. A glance over the shoulder showed the half-breed that a scowling George was behind him.

'You turned down a job I was prepared to offer you,' Ryan continued, drawing against his pipe with contentment. 'Man has a right to do that. It's a free country.'

'Some folks are freer than others,' Edge replied, sharing a glance between his two beefy captors. Only the weighty giants were close enough to read a threat into the glance. But, in their present position, they could afford to grin in response.

The rancher ignored the wry comment. 'Knowin' what a hothead my brother-in-law and foreman is, I'll even allow you was provoked to turn down the job in the way you did.' He shrugged and stared reflectively out across the quietly gliding water of the river which made his valley such a green and pleasant strip of country. 'But Harv's popular with the boys and they don't take kindly to how you altered his looks.'

'Can we start on in now, Mr Ryan?' George asked eagerly.

'Hold on,' the rancher insisted and looked hard at Edge through the blue smoke curling from his pipe bowl. 'I just want to make my position clear to you, Edge. You're the kind of man I admire. You got guts and you can handle yourself. You did a good job gettin' to Greenville and I'd have been happy to have you work for me. But you didn't want to. And neither did you want to work for folks fixin' to go against me. So you and me got no quarrel. Except over the matter of your dead horse. But, when the boys here are through with you, you'll get the best mount we got here. And they're all good.'

His dark eyes requested a response. 'Then we got no quarrel at all, feller,' Edge said.

Ryan nodded his satisfaction. 'Just one more thing – to steer clear of any chance of misunderstanding. I said my piece not on account of I'm scared by you, Edge. But you're a drifter. A saddletramp. You move around. Just want to be sure that, when you talk about me, you let folks know I'm a fair man. What's goin' to happen now is somethin' between you and Harv London's buddies. If things get out of hand and they look set to kill you, I'll stop them. That sound fair to you, Edge?'

The half-breed spat. At nobody. Just down between the toe-caps of his own boots. 'You got the pack, feller,' he answered. 'And I ain't in no position to argue with the deal.'

Ryan's gaze wandered out across the river again. 'Do what you have to, boys,' he invited.

George was a quiet mover. He had approached to within reach of Edge at the back. Edge wasn't aware of it until a punch thudded into his kidneys. Harding and Carver staged the distraction, inching in close at the front. The giants did not move. A grunt was vented from Edge's throat as the impact of the bunched fist arched his body forward. Harding and Carver shed their diversionary roles and become a full frontal attack. The taller, blond hand swung a left. The dark-eyed Carver threw a right in tandem. Both fists made simultaneous contact. Low down at either side of Edge's belly. The new sound forced from the half-breed's lips was the woosh of escaping air. His body was driven backwards this time, on the pivots of his shoulder joints while the giants held his arms utterly still.

With an almost girlish giggle, George stepped forward and brought up his knee. It smashed into Edge's crotch from behind.

'How about that?' George shrieked.

Edge's feet were lifted clear of the ground by the force of the impact. Agony demanded vocal outlet from two new sources as the giants held him rock steady and his arms threatened to be torn from their sockets.

'He dances good!' one of the watchers yelled.

'And if he sings it'll be soprano!' another countered.

Edge heard the voices at normal level. He could even hear the steady breathing of his captors and the faster, excited respiration of the three men delivering the beating. His hooded eyes received vivid images of the men in front of him, the mutilated corpses spread on the ground and the backdrop of timber, river and grassland. His sense of feel was as potent as ever.

When he slammed back down to his feet, the jarring pain

rose from his ankles to the top of his skull, sharpening the agonies in his belly, his crotch, at the base of his spine and across his shoulders. Another pair of punches from Harding and Carver smacked into the hard ridges of muscles at his belly. But the flesh was not tough enough to protect the nerve-endings behind it. Pain exploded like a starshell, red hot fragments scything through him to every part of his body. A grunt and warm saliva spilled from his lips.

'Yeah, you got guts all right, snot-nose!' Carver taunted.

'And they'll be spillin' out through your ass when we're through with you!' Harding snarled.

The pattern was maintained. As the two men at the front arched the half-breed's body backwards, the one at the rear attacked. George used his fist and knee at the same time. The knee went wide and cracked against Edge's thigh. But the blow with his hand struck home. The half-breed had been able to hold his head erect – until George's work-toughened knuckles smashed into the back of his neck. Then Edge's head fell forward and he screwed his eyes tight against the pain. When he snapped them open and brought his head up again, all the previously clear images were blurred.

But the pain was as well defined as ever. Voices were yelling and screaming but he couldn't understand the words. Could not even be sure the voices were not inside his head. People shrieking at him from out of his memory.

Jamie Hedges, his brother.

Carver caught Edge in the throat with a heel-of-the-hand chop.

Elizabeth.

Harding landed a fist against the victim's heart.

Bob Rhett.

George smashed a toecap into the back of the right knee joint.

Sergeant Frank Forrest.

'Lower!' somebody shouted.

The giants eased out of their rigidity. They maintained their vice-like holds on arms and wrists. Edge sagged under his own weight to rest on his knees. If he had not been held up, he would have collapsed into a heap.

Pike. Seward. Bell. John Scott. Corporal Douglas.

George caught hold of two fistfuls of the half-breed's long

hair and hauled. The head was forced up.

Cheering. Not from out of the past. Though the men whose names had flipped through the pain-assaulted mind would have cheered.

Harding smashed a fist into the exposed and defenceless face. The hair was almost yanked out of George's hands, but he held on, shrieking his delight.

Everyone except Jamie and Elizabeth would have cheered if they could have witnessed this beating. But none of them could. They were all dead. Edge had not killed all of them. Most.

Carver hit him and the tough skin split where it curved tautly over the cheekbone. Harding's fist split the corner of the mouth.

Edge heard somebody groaning and knew it had to be him. It, and the dull thud of flesh against flesh were the only sounds he could hear now. Everything beyond his own existence afloat in a sea of bright crimson pain was too far off for him to experience. He felt the warm stickiness of blood sheening his face. There was warmth and moisture coating every plane of his body, but this would be sweat.

Numbness spread a merciful sensation of well-being through him. He had reached that far limit of agony where nothing they could do to him would cause him further pain. At this moment. His nervous system had been overloaded by punishment and had shut down because it could take no more.

He felt and heard the fists hitting him but the feeling in the impacts was as blunted as the sounds were distant. They became blunter and further away. He guessed there was blood in his nostrils and in his throat because he seemed to be drowning in a deep pool of warm wetness. He could not hear himself making any more sounds.

He was not aware when the two giants unfastened their big hands from around his arms and wrists. He did not feel himself fall to the side and he expected to hear a splash. Night dew on the lush grass sprinkled his punished face and its freshness and coolness held him back from plunging over the brink into unconsciousness.

A toecap smashed with tremendous force into the centre of his chest and the pain it exploded was powerful enough to put sharpness on all the others.

'Hey, George, you never oughta kick a man when he's down!'

Edge heard this comment clearly. Also the burst of laughter that followed it. He thought he replied: 'Because here's one that's sure gonna get up again, feller.' But, if he didn't say it, he thought it. And meant it.

'Enough!' another voice bellowed. Familiar. Pike? Jamie? Forrest? Bell? None of them. A man with a beard and neat clothes. Ryan. Woodrow Ryan.

'Okay, Mr Ryan,' a voice confirmed. 'I guess we're through with this snot-nose. Paid him out good for what he done to Harv, didn't we?'

'The odds were entirely in your favour, Carver,' the big rancher said. Even through his pain, Edge thought he detected a note of regret in the rich voice. 'When he speaks of you on his travels, the word fair will not spring to his mind.'

'I never speak ill of the dead.'

Edge knew he had definitely uttered this comment aloud. His voice was croaky and wet-sounding. The sudden, tense silence that greeted the words was confirmation they had been heard.

'Hey, this tough nut's still awake. You hear what he said, Mr Ryan? You want we should do it some more?'

'I told you enough, George!' Ryan barked. He raised his voice: 'Edge, if you can hear me, listen good. Fair warnin' from a fair man. Don't make futile threats. You're not comin' back to this valley. If you show your battered features here again, you'll be killed on sight.'

There was another silence, but it wasn't words which ended it this time. Edge sucked in painful lungfuls of air to power a response. But the beating finally had its inevitable effect. As he opened his mouth to speak, his mind plunged him into a pit of blackness where nothing existed except bad dreams that would never be remembered.

George crouched at the half-breed's side and rolled him over on to his back. Limp arms and legs swung without resistance.

'He's passed out now, for sure, Mr Ryan,' the stockily-built hand reported. 'Man, what a mess he's in!'

'Hey, you sound almost sorry for that guy,' one of the giants taunted.

George rose with a grin. 'He don't need that from me. When he wakes up, he's gonna be plenty sorry for himself.'

'Give him back his weapons and tie him to your horse!'
Ryan instructed sternly. 'You'll ride back with somebody else.'

'What about these, Mr Ryan?' Harding asked, waving a
bruised hand to encompass the shattered corpses of the farmers.

'May not even be our problem,' the rancher answered. 'Don't
know if this is my land or not until the survey's been made.'

'So we just leave 'em here?' Carver asked.

'You have somethin' else in mind, Carver?'

Harding laughed. 'Hell, Mr Ryan. Carver don't even have a
mind.'

Carver joined in the laughter. 'I sure had a mind to give
the snot-nose what was comin' to him.'

Chapter Four

PAIN was no longer a sea washing over Edge in waves. It was a series of hammers thudding against his flesh and through it to strike at his bones and his vital organs. Each hammer was raised and smashed down onto him in perfect unison. The battering had the same cadence and rhythm of a galloping horse. And the sound was the same, too: counterpointing the groans and gasps which the beating forced from his throat.

He opened his eyes and the lids caught fire. He stared into red heat. The burning merged with all the other agonies engulfing his body and his vision cleared. The crimson colour retreated and he saw a blurred, rushing panorama of black and grey. The constant pain exploding at every nerve ending tried to block his mind from thinking of any other aspect of his existence. But the half-breed knew pain of old and had learned long ago how to handle it. Not by ignoring it. That was impossible. But it could be accepted.

Accepted with self-pity, if a man was a fool and a coward. Like Bob Rhett . . . He rejected this name. It came from too far out of the past.

Ryan. Harding. Carver. A man named George. These were the names he at last managed to drag from his memory and thrust into the forefront of his tenuous consciousness. Hatred. That was the way to handle pain. Deep-seated, bitter hatred towards those who had inflicted the punishment. Allied with a determination to avenge what they had done. In such a way could a man accept his present condition and resolve to recover from it — in order to inflict even greater punishment upon those who attacked him.

The thirst for vengeance battled with the fires of agony in Edge's mind. For a long time his mind twisted and turned through the labyrinthine passages of the conflicting emotions and his eyes were closed again. The black and the grey were gone and the insides of his eyelids showed the former crimson. But the colour was no longer even. The backdrop swirled and broiled and different shades of the same colour advanced and retreated.

Edge knew he was on a horse. Recalled the promise of the man named Ryan. Draped over the saddle of the horse and tied there. The blur of black and grey when he opened his eyes was his upside-down view of the country at night as the horse galloped across it. That accounted for the regular beat of the pain. As each hoof of the bolting horse hit the ground, it jarred every punished muscle and every battered area of flesh of the man upon its back.

He didn't know whether his face showed a bitter grin. Was aware only that he felt the need to express a degree of satisfaction. His defence against pain was working. By remembering names and events of the recent past, he had forced his reluctant mind to accept useful logic rather than indulge in futile self-pity. He did not know precisely where he was, but he knew how he had got there.

He was unaware of time. It was still night. The same night of the beating. The speed of the bolting horse told him that. And the degree of his own agony. If that night had ended and an entire day had passed, the horse would be exhausted and his pain would have lost its sharpness.

The hammer blows assaulting him slowed in pace. The muscles of his back were thrust harder against the restraining ropes that held him across the saddle. He continued to stare into the variegated crimson of his inner eyelids and sensed that the horse was slowing and turning.

Edge trusted broke horses. Horse-sense was no mere smart phrase thought up out of the air by a smart mouth. It was horses which were the smart ones. They knew how to stay out of trouble. Ryan claimed he bred only the best kind and Edge had good reason to trust the man's word on this. It was a good bet that well-bred horses were also well trained.

The punished man consciously shook his head: as opposed to having it swung from side to side by the jolting progress of the animal beneath him. His mind was wandering back to Ryan and that was not necessary any more. The rancher and his hard-fisted hands had served their purpose for now. The half-breed knew he was going to pull through: providing the horse didn't plunge over a cliff, break a leg on rough ground or try for a river crossing in the wrong place.

And he had to trust the horse not to do any of these things. For his body was way behind his mind in overcoming the gruelling effects of pain. His mind was equal to the task of telling him he should halt the horse, untie himself from it and get his bearings. But the effort of simply shaking his head used up more strength than he thought he had.

The horse stopped, and gave out a whinny that trembled through its entire body. Edge heard the trickling of water and the sound emphasised the acrid taste of congealed blood in his mouth.

'Danny! Danny! Come quickly!'

The woman's voice reached Edge's ears. It seemed like many hours after the horse had stopped to drink, but he did not trust such a guess. Time still had no meaning. He may have blacked out. Perhaps only for a second or two. He could hear the horse sucking up water. Taking the same drink from the same water? . . . Or another drink from someplace else?

He heard footfalls, the tread light and padding across soft ground.

'What's wrong, Maria?'

A man's voice. Danny? From a long way off. The horse backed up and gave another whinny. Nervous sounding this time. The woman spoke softly. In a language Edge understood but had not spoken for many years. The Spanish tongue of the Mexicans, such as his father had sometimes spoken. Maria was telling the horse not to be afraid. That it was all right and nothing was going to hurt it. The animal responded by standing still. Maria moved closer. Edge could hear her clothes rustling as she walked. Then he smelled her. She smelled good. Fresh, clean, feminine. No perfume. The natural smell of a woman after she had bathed.

She sucked in her breath sharply. When she expelled it, the air powered a scream.

'Maria!'

Danny was closer. The shrill tone in which he shrieked the name held all the anguish in the world. His footfalls thudded in a flat out sprint. The scream ended and Maria began to breath rapidly, as if she was experiencing the same exertion as Danny.

Edge opened his eyes and the multi-hued crimson vanished. The world was no longer grey and black. For a moment it remained blurred, then his vision cleared. He saw Maria first. Squatting on the ground and staring at him through horror-widened eyes. She was about twenty-two or three with a slender body clothed in a simple pink dress that was stained and patched and torn. She had jet black hair, cropped short which clung to her head like a tight-fitting hat. Her face was darkened by heritage, its features even and pretty. Ordinary and lacking character.

He saw her in the light of sunrise. The harsh yellow of the new day's birth pangs showed him other things – beyond where the woman squatted. The bank of the river from which the horse had drank. A broad meadow with some grazing sheep and a milk cow. On the far side of the meadow was a small, crudely built shack with a larger barn at the side. At the side of the barn was a corral with a half dozen horses in it. The man was streaking across the meadow on a diagonal line from the barn to where the horse, Edge and Maria were waiting. The half-breed caught only a glimpse of him before his eyelids grew too heavy and he was looking into the crimson pool again. At least that was the right way up – if there was a right and a wrong way. The images of reality he had seen were all inverted: viewed upside-down from beneath the curved belly of the horse.

'Who are you?' Maria asked in English. 'What has happened to you?'

'Maria!' Danny yelled, less anxious now that he could see his wife.

Was it his wife? Edge didn't know. He simply made the assumption. And immediately he dismissed the doubt as unimportant. He never liked accepting help. It wasn't his way. Favours demanded favours in return, even if such responses were not invited. But he needed help now. More than he had ever needed it in his life before.

'I was with the wrong people at the wrong time, ma'am,' he heard himself say, without recognising the croaking note in his own voice.

Danny stopped running and drew gasping breaths. He had to force out the words. 'Maria? Are you all right? Who is he? Where did he come from? Is he dead?' He was an American.

'That was three other fellers,' the half-breed croaked, and managed to snap open his eyes again.

Danny was squatting down beside Maria, with an arm draped over her shoulders. He was in the same age group as the woman and dressed in work-worn levis, dusty boots and check shirt. He had a mop of red, curly hair above a freckled face. At some time he had suffered a broken nose. His eyes were pale brown. There was strength in his face and his compact body looked as if it was host to a lot of power.

He drew back a little as Edge spoke, and looked as frightened as Maria. But then it passed. 'Man, are you in a mess!' he rasped.

'It can't look any worse than it feels, feller,' Edge answered.

'Danny, we must get him off the horse and into the house,' Maria said, recovered from her own horror and now just anxious.

'Obliged for the thought, ma'am,' the half-breed said, closing his eyes. 'But it ain't always just the thought that counts.'

Edge blacked out again.

Daniel Oakley and his bride of three weeks backed the thought with the deed. They led the sweat-lathered horse and its unconscious rider up the slope of the meadow to the front of the small shack. A fire was already curling smoke from the chimney and the pretty young Mexican woman went inside to put water on the stove to boil. Her husband hitched the reins of the weary gelding to the tail-gate of a buckboard and used a knife to saw through the ropes which held Edge to the saddle. There were two of them. One looped under his belt and lashed to the saddlehorn. The second, longer length bound a leg to one stirrup and an arm to the other.

The young Oakley displayed his strength then, by the manner in which he lifted the unconscious dead weight of Edge off the horse and carried him inside the house. There were just two spartanly furnished but scrupulously clean rooms inside. Maria was busy at the stove in the kitchen section of the main room and her husband moved across and into the bedroom. The bed was already made and he gently lowered his weighty burden onto the patchwork quilted cover. For the first time, he was able to see and study the face of the stranger from a normal viewpoint and he reacted with a grimace. Maria entered the bedroom silently, until she announced her presence with a gasp.

'He could die, I reckon,' Danny said grimly.

'*Madre de Dios!*' his wife whispered, and crossed herself.

If Edge had had friends, it was unlikely any of them would have recognised him as he lay on the bed, breathing as if every intake of air would be his last. His features were a nightmarish parody of the human face. There was not one section of flesh which was normal. A mass of swellings were coloured blue and purple. This where the blood from ugly splits and bursts had not run and congealed to black. The worst bruising was around the eyes which looked incapable of ever opening again. The most blood had come from the nostrils and the wounds made by teeth sinking into the swollen lips. It was this which was making his breathing so laboured.

Tentatively, Danny stooped and began to unfasten the buttons of the blood-stained shirt and the red undershirt beneath. Because nothing could be so terrible to look at as the battered face, the discoloured bruises on the torso drew no further reactions of horror from the couple.

'Is there anything we can do, Danny?' Maria asked earnestly. 'Should you ride to El Paso for a doctor?'

'We can't afford a doctor,' her husband pointed out.

'He may have money.'

The man shook his head.

Maria nodded. 'No, of course not. Men so evil as to do this would take anything of value he had. So we must do what we can.'

And the Oakleys did what they could for the tall, lean stranger who did not regain consciousness while they cleaned his wounds, bathed his bruises and applied salve and dressings. They could do no more than this, knowing only enough to tend the visible injuries. They could not diagnose internal damage.

But they were hopeful for the results of their crude medical treatment. The man was resting easy and breathing more naturally when the young couple left the bedroom to resume the chores around their small homestead. No longer worried about the health of the stranger, Danny and Maria had time to consider their initial anxieties about him. Who he was and why he had been so brutally beaten? And these anxieties were heightened when, as he unsaddled the tan gelding in the barn, Danny saw the Big R brand on the animal.

Like every other farmer and homesteader in the valley, Danny and his bride had good reason to hate and fear Woodrow Ryan. They had inherited the place from Danny's newly dead father and with the land had come the responsibility to share its income with the man who claimed he owned every square inch of the valley. So far, the new owners had not been faced with the humiliating reality of their true position as tenants working another man's land. They had been in San Antonio when they got word of the older Oakley's death and bequest. An attorney in El Paso had read them the will and had then advised them of the position adopted by Woodrow Ryan.

With each of the twenty-one days that had passed since they arrived after their marriage in El Paso, Danny and Maria had expected the next to bring a visit from Ryan men. But none had come so far. The only people they had seen were reluctant tenants like themselves, moving back and forth between their homesteads and the stores and merchants in El Paso. All of them had confirmed what the attorney said. And all of them warned the newcomers to the valley against resistance to Ryan's will. He had the legal papers and, if these were not accepted, he had the men to enforce the rights he claimed.

As he came out of the barn after attending to the stranger's horse, Danny considered keeping the matter of the Big R brand to himself. But he rejected it immediately. Maria and he had kept no secrets from each other before they were married and had vowed to continue with this code when they became man and wife. So he went into the house where she was preparing breakfast and he told her.

'Does that not mean he is a Ryan man?' the woman asked as she set a plate of bacon and eggs in front of her husband.

'Unless he bought or stole the horse,' Danny replied.

Maria could not face eating after seeing the terrible injuries of the man sleeping in the next room. She sat down across the table from her husband with just a tin mug of coffee. 'It does not matter who he is!' she said emphatically after long moments of silence. 'He was hurt and in need of help.' She glanced up at the crucifix which was the room's sole ornament. 'It was our duty to aid him.'

Danny's freckled face showed earnestness, then he nodded his agreement. 'That is absolutely right, Maria,' he said emphatically. 'Who he is and what he did to earn the beating is none of our concern. Nor is the horse he was ridin'. We only did what any decent human beings would do.'

A wan smile turned up the corners of the woman's full mouth. She reached out across the table and gripped her husband's hand lightly. 'But it is not ill-will to wish him quickly recovered and gone from here, I think?'

Danny nodded again, but with less resolution. He glanced over his shoulder to the closed doorway which gave on to the bedroom. 'Though if he was well and not a Ryan man, I wouldn't mind him being here when the Big R hands show up, Maria. He's big and he's strong and he's tough. And mean with it, I'd guess.'

'Danny!' Maria said crossly, withdrawing her hand. 'You promised. Your father worked this land and paid Ryan. You promised we would try to do the same before causing trouble.'

Now it was the husband's turn to reach out and clasp his wife's hand. His smile was brighter than hers had been. 'Just daydreaming, Maria,' he promised. 'You remember – we said we would never get married unless we had our own piece of land. Life cheated us, *mi bien*. I was just thinking that, with a man like that one . . . we could perhaps – '

'An army of men like him would be needed,' Maria cut in, and her free hand reached out to cup his. 'And even then, they say that Ryan has many to help him.' She glanced at the closed door and shuddered. 'He might even be one of them.'

With this possibility re-established, a mood of gloom insinuated itself into the tiny house. Breakfast was hurriedly finished and the Oakleys sought to forget about the stranger by plunging themselves into the work of the small farm: going about their chores today as they would have done each day had the land been their own.

It was Jack Clayton who told them of last night's trouble when he drove his buckboard to a halt at the side of the spur trail that cut diagonally across the Oakley homestead to join the El Paso trail. The middle-aged Clayton and his painfully thin wife were both grim faced and pale as they watched Danny and Maria emerge from the barn. Maria turned towards the house after giving a wave of greeting, intent upon sharing mid-morning coffee with the Claytons.

'Won't be able to keep anythin' in our stomachs for awhile, Mrs Oakley,' Clayton called. 'Just stopped by to tell you somethin' you oughta know about.'

The Oakleys were immediately anxious, first catching the bitter tones of the man, then seeing the grave expressions on the faces of their distant neighbours. The newly-weds clasped hands as they approached the heavily-laden buckboard. Its high-stacked load of hay provided a patch of shade in the hot morning sun.

'Was killing up beyond the Crosby place last night,' Clayton announced as his wife stared blankly into place. Marilla was usually the most light-hearted of women. 'Yates, Selby and Kelsey. Kinda hard to recognise them.'

'Blown into pieces,' Marilla intoned.

'With a shotgun,' her husband explained.

Maria gasped and pressed closer to Danny. The young couple stared up at the man on the buckboard seat, waiting for more.

'Don't know the whys and wherefores,' Clayton continued. 'But it's common knowledge Ryan favours carrying a shotgun.'

'Paid us a visit last night,' Marilla said, as vague as before.

'She means the three that were killed,' Clayton supplemented. 'Told us they had news from Greenville. Stranger in town mixed it with some of Ryan's hands. Handled them like they was day-old lambs and rode out. Yates and Selby and Kelsey — they figured to meet up with this stranger and hire him to go against the Ryan set-up. I told them I didn't want no part of that.'

'I told him to tell them that,' Marilla put in, and now she looked intently at the young couple. 'Reason he's alive this mornin' and not spread over the grass at Rivertrees Bend.'

Maria tore her stare away from the harrowed eyes of the other woman and showed Danny an imploring expression.

'That's terrible, Mr Clayton,' was all Danny said.

'Somethin' else you ought to know, young feller. Had some callers this morning. Two city types with a map and survey equipment. And a couple of real mean-lookin' bast . . . fellers.

48

Ryan's kinda men, but I ain't never seen them before. Seems Ryan's figurin' to make his claim to the valley real hide-bound. Don't mess with them, young feller.'

'Tell Danny, Maria,' the older woman advised earnestly, the shock of seeing the corpses still with her but the vagueness gone. 'His father was like us and all the other folk here. We lived at peace with Ryan and we got by. Soon as this stranger showed up, there was pain and killin'.'

Clayton released the brake of the buckboard and flicked the reins.

'Danny!' Maria implored.

He squeezed her hand. 'Thanks for stoppin' by to tell us, Mr Clayton,' he called as the wagon started forward.

'Don't mess with them, son!' the older man called.

'Just do like they say,' Marilla Clayton added.

'It is him!' Maria said, soft but intent, so that the creaking and clopping progress of the departing buckboard covered her words. 'He is the stranger, Danny!'

The young man nodded his agreement and there was just the trace of a grim smile at the corners of his mouth. When he moved, still clasping the hand of his wife, Maria was forced to follow him. He led her into the house and across the main room to the closed door. He opened it quietly and the two of them stood on the threshold. Danny looked at the sleeping man with interested curiosity. Maria's eyes were as horror-filled as when she had first seen Edge's upside-down face under the belly of the gelding.

'See him as a warning,' the woman begged. 'He bettered the Ryan men once. And see how he paid for it, Danny.'

'I'm lookin', *mi bien*,' Danny replied evenly. 'And, when he wakes up, he'll look at himself. And feel the pain. A man like he is, Maria. Do you think he'll just ride away and forget what they did to him?'

'Danny, I don't care about him!' Maria said, and her voice was almost a high-pitched scream.

Edge groaned and moved an arm, but he did not recover consciousness. Danny expressed annoyance at his wife and hustled her out of the bedroom, closing the door. 'He's goin' to be all right,' he said, immediately regretting his flash of anger. 'But he'll need plenty of rest.' He kissed his wife lightly on the cheek and his smile held genuine affection as he withdrew from her. 'Make some coffee, Maria. And I promise not to say anything more about him until he wakes up.'

'But you will think about him,' the woman accused.

The smile brightened still further. 'As the stranger said, *mi bien*: it isn't the thought that counts.'

The Oakleys were just finishing their coffee, drinking it in the shade of the house stoop, when the four riders approached along the spur trail. They heard the hoofbeats first, coming from beyond the stand of trees that formed the northern boundary of the homestead. The trail curved around the timber and emerged into sight on the bank of the river which marked the extent of the property on the eastern side. Not that property markers meant anything in the valley except those staking the Big R claim.

The riders appeared on the river bank just short of where Maria had first seen the gelding with the beaten man tied to it. But the quartet of newcomers required no help. Instead of staying on the trail which made a right angle turn to skirt the trees, they swung across the lush meadow, scattering the sheep and causing the milk cow to lumber out of their path as they galloped up the slope.

'It is them!' Maria said nervously as she and Danny got to their feet. 'Please do as Mr Clayton advised.'

Once again, she reached for his hand and clasped it, as the four riders reined their mounts to a halt, and lined up before the house.

'Good morning, ma'am. Sir. You must be Mr and Mrs Oakley.' The speaker was a tall, thin man attired in a city suit of blue serge, a brown derby and a white shirt with ruffled collar. He touched the brim of his hat politely and showed tobacco stained teeth when his bloodless lips parted in a smile. He had soft, brown eyes with dark circles under them. 'Name's Finbar. This is my associate from San Francisco. Mr Standish.'

'It certainly is a fine morning,' Standish said. He had a strong British accent. A head shorter than Finbar, he was just as thin as the other man. He was also dressed in a suit, but it was grey. The same as his derby hat. At thirty, he was ten years junior to Finbar. Weakly handsome, he wore a thin moustache above his full mouth. He took off his hat and showed a mop of black hair, as if to compensate for his associate's apparent baldness. His smile was a trifle nervous.

'Fellers come to do a survey.

'We're here to see they don't get no trouble while they're doin' it.'

Finbar's smile almost fell off his face, but he managed to rescue it. 'Mr Royd and Mr Doyle. Our employer, Mr Woodrow Ryan of the Big R Ranch, insisted these gentlemen accompanied us.' He even brightened his smile now, as Standish's nervousness increased. 'Though we are certain you will be as co-operative as the other tenants we have visited.'

Royd was in his early twenties. He was stockily built and had a squarish face chiselled into lines of sullenness. His brooding, dark eyes had hardly left Maria Oakley since he halted his horse. Doyle was a few years older and a great deal better looking. But the pleasantness of his features was not matched by the gravel tones of his voice. He was about six feet tall and heavier than he should have been, for his belly bulged and hung over the top of his pants. Both Royd and Doyle were attired Western-style and were armed with holstered sixguns and booted rifles. They sat their saddles with easy comfort. The two surveyors showed no weapons and looked in danger of falling from their mounts.

'What kind of survey?' Danny asked, with a slight tremor in his voice. 'Just of my wife?'

Royd completed his arrogant appraisal of Maria's face and figure and swung his dark eyes towards Danny. His lips curled back. 'Takin' account of land and stock, mister. That's a nice lookin' filly you got there.'

Finbar and Standish were in the process of dismounting, expressing relief to get from their saddles. But Finbar became stern as he heard the comment and saw Danny Oakley's face colour with anger.

'Mr Royd!' the surveyor snapped. 'Bear in mind Mr Ryan's instructions.'

Standish looked ready to turn and run as Royd transferred his leer towards Finbar and altered it slightly, into a sneer.

'Attend to your business, dude,' the guard growled. 'Just complimentin' the pretty little Mex girl is all.'

'Easy, Jamie!' Doyle warned, sliding from his saddle. 'That rancher feller give me the impression he don't just talk to hear himself.'

'Aw, hell!' Royd whined, and spat as he dismounted. 'This is sure some lousy job you got us into, John.'

'Pays better than the El Paso crap tables,' Doyle pointed out. When he smiled, it went some way to discounting his harsh-sounding voice. The smile was for Maria and there seemed to be no hidden meaning behind it. He took off his hat to show neatly clipped and slicked down sandy hair. 'If there's any coffee left in the pot, ma'am, I for one would sure appreciate a cup.'

Maria shot a glance at Danny and received a nod of assent.

'Mr Standish and I may take up that kind invitation later,' Finbar said quickly, his brightness an over-reaction to the defusing of the situation. 'After we've finished our work.'

'It surely is a hot day for work,' Standish said, licking beads of sweat off his moustache.

'Damn right it is!' Royd growled, and delved into one of his saddlebags. A grin spread across his weathered face as he produced a bottle of whisky. 'Coffee's for friggin' cold nights. I got what's needed for friggin' hot days.'

Maria spun and went into the house, carrying the mugs she and Danny had used. The two surveyors were in the process of unloading their equipment from their horses. A lower-keyed anger spread over the face of the young homesteader.

'I object to swearin' in front of my wife!' he complained.

'Weren't in front of her, mister!' Royd answered, still grinning. 'It was behind her.' He uncapped the bottle, took a swig and laughed. 'And I can't recall the last time I saw a prettier behind.'

Danny made to step off the stoop, glaring at Royd. Doyle shot out a hand, the palm and splayed fingers pressing hard into the centre of Danny's chest.

'Our boss told us no trouble,' the tall gunman said, his no longer smiling eyes boring into Danny's face. 'That we start. Our boss hired us to stop trouble anyone else starts.'

. Finbar and Standish hurried to unpack their gear, then went at a half-run down the slope of the meadow towards the river bank. They didn't look back, as if afraid of what they might see.

Danny held Doyle's stare for long moments. And, in the other man's eyes, he read the fact that Doyle was more dangerous than his stockier partner. 'Just keep him out of sight and earshot of my wife then!' the homesteader rasped.

'Hey, John!' Royd snarled. 'That punk givin' us orders?'

'Easy, Jamie,' Doyle called over his shoulder, then returned his attention to Danny as Maria emerged on to the stoop with a mug of steaming coffee. 'Appreciate it, ma'am,' he said, accepting the mug. There was no smile. He lowered his voice. 'Advise you both to stay inside the house. Ain't no reason for any of us to come in there.'

'Why should – ' Danny started.

Doyle's voice stayed at a low level, but it became a snarl. 'Listen, you crazy country boy! Jamie Royd and me been partners a long time. I know him. And I can handle him if I get the chance. But if he gets to see too much of your wife, or you say the wrong word, ain't no one can handle him. You get me, country boy?'

Danny looked over one of Doyle's shoulders while Maria was more fleeting in her survey of the other one. Both saw Royd clearly, sucking from the whisky bottle and raking his gaze over the homestead, by turns grinning and scowling.

'We will do as you say,' the woman agreed, and at once turned and went into the house.

Danny seemed about to protest, but his angry eyes were again captured by Doyle's cold and revealing stare. 'Just keep him away from Maria and me,' he said before he whirled and followed his wife inside. He slammed the door hard behind him.

'Hey, John,' Royd slurred, draping an arm around Doyle's waist as the taller man got close to him. The bottle had been half empty when he took it from the saddlebag. He had been taking regular swallows from it throughout the morning.

'Yeah, Jamie?' Doyle asked, sipping the coffee and steering his partner towards the promised shade of the barn.

'That damn Britisher, all he talks about is the weather.'

'That's 'cause, the way I hear it, the British have such lousy stuff.' He succeeded in moving Royd onto course for the barn. 'Can't get over what we got.'

'But all he does is complain about it, John,' Royd argued.

The whites of his eyes were already bloodshot. He squinted as he peered around, searching for the surveyors. He spotted them, down on the bank of the river, at either end of a long measuring tape. Beyond them, the slow running water looked cool and inviting as it sparkled in the sunlight.

'We don't have to listen to him or the other city feller,' Doyle reminded. 'Just guard them is all.'

'Guess that's right,' Royd acknowledged, and took another swig of whisky. The two men reached the threshold of the barn. In the shade of the doorway, the smaller man broke contact with the larger one. He turned, and stood swaying as he peered down the sloping meadow at the river. 'But you was sure listening to that punk and his Mex woman, John. What'd they say? And what did you say back?'

He swung around suddenly, and stared suspiciously up into the face of his partner. Doyle stayed cool in response to Royd's aggressive attitude.

'We made a deal, Jamie. Remember? In El Paso after we took this job. We said no booze and no women until it was over and we got paid. I gave way on the booze, Jamie. But don't you get no idea of making a play for that woman. She's the feller's wife.'

Royd sneered, then mellowed the expression into a grin. 'All the better, John partner. She knows what it's for and what it's all about.'

Doyle finished his coffee and sighed. 'Please, Jamie,' he asked softly and now there was nothing in his face to suggest toughness or danger. The look he had given Danny, to clinch the homesteader's retreat into the house, had been a sham. Royd, drunk or sober, was the dominant one of the partnership. And this was patently evident as the two men stood in the doorway of the barn. 'When we done this job, we'll have enough money to buy any women we want.'

Royd shook his head, still holding the grin, and thrust the almost empty bottle towards Doyle. 'Bought women are used too many times, John.' He hitched up his gunbelt. 'And virgins are just too much trouble. Ain't nothin' I like better than a new bride.'

Doyle sighed again. 'I can't talk you outta this, Jamie?'

'You and me ain't much for talk, John.'

Doyle thought about this, nodded, and raised the bottle to his lips. He tilted it and drained it of the hefty slug of whisky it contained. 'That sure is right, Jamie.'

Royd laughed harshly. 'So you'll watch them city slickers keep right on with their work, John?'

'If it's gotta be this way.'

Royd stepped out of the barn. 'When a man's got it hard, only one natural thing to do, John.'

'Lean on a crutch, Jamie,' Doyle countered, following his partner outside and drawing his Colt.

'Right, John. Aw hell, I can hardly wait. Them Mex fillies always give a feller a good ride. And this one's new broke in.'

Chapter Five

'HEY, Jamie! Don't you wear her out, partner. I figure I'll have some of what she's got!'

On the outer shore of returning consciousness, Edge heard the familiar name called. Perhaps he heard the rest of the words yelled by the gravel-voiced John Doyle. But he didn't understand them. Just the name Jamie. He smiled in the last remnant of his unnatural sleep and was suddenly painfully awake. For it was as if his face caught fire as his muscles tugged at the punished flesh to form the smile.

Danny Oakley had been at the front window of the shack's main room, looking towards the barn doorway where Royd and Doyle stood talking. As the smaller gunman staggered out into the sunlight and Doyle followed him, drawing the revolver, the young homesteader groaned.

'What is it?' Maria asked anxiously, moving fast from the stove to the window to look out.

'Go into the bedroom, Maria,' her husband told her forcefully. 'And if there's trouble, get through the window and run. Run as fast and as far as you can.'

Anxiety became terror as the woman looked around the man and saw the leering Royd as he neared the house.

'Do as I say!' Danny commanded, giving her a shove towards the bedroom door as he turned from the window.

Her big, dark, fear-widened eyes followed him as he crossed the room and took a Winchester rifle from where it leaned against the wall in the corner.

'Hey, mister!' Royd yelled. 'Send that Mex woman of yours out here, will you?'

Danny's own fear, larded with anger, was too allconsuming. He was unable to soften his expression as he stared at his wife after pumping the rifle's action. And his voice was as harsh as the look on his face.

'Do as I told you!' he snarled.

She had never seen him like this. Had never heard him use such a tone. Would never have dreamed he would look at her and talk to her in such a way. Tears spilled from her wide eyes and a sob was wrenched from her throat as she whirled. Then, as her trembling hand wrapped around the handle, a faint hope sprang into her mind. She remembered the man who was on the other side of the door: recalled what Danny had thought about him.

'What on earth . . . ?' a British voice exclaimed.

'You men!' the other surveyor called.

Their voices were faint, coming from the other side of the meadow.

'Keep on working!' Doyle ordered, from much nearer the house.

Maria pushed open the door and stepped quickly into the bedroom. The sob became a gasp as she closed the door and leaned her back against it. Blue slits of eyes stared across the room at her from the wreckage of the stranger's face.

'Men!' she hissed. 'Making trouble for Danny and me! Please help us!'

It was as painful for Edge to talk as to smile. But he managed to croak a reply. 'It ain't that I'm unmoved, ma'am,' he told the anguished woman. 'Just that I can't.'

Danny Oakley was too slow. He had spent time checking the rifle and ensuring that his wife was through into the bedroom. Only then did he make for his former vantage point at the window. Jamie Royd's moves were far quicker, despite his drunken state. After shouting the demand to Danny, he had lengthened his stride and set his feet down silently. So, when the young homesteader peered out through the freshly laundered lace curtains and polished glass, he failed to spot Royd. He saw Doyle midway between the barn and the house, holding his gun negligently. He saw Finbar and Standish on the river bank, staring up towards the house. He saw the four horses waiting patiently immediately outside the house.

The groan which Danny vented this time had a note of desperation in it. He leaned closer to the window, to widen his angle of vision. Glass shattered behind him and he started to whirl. A man laughed and a gunshot exploded. Danny froze, in mid-turn, as the window he had been looking through was smashed by a bullet.

'Drop the rifle, punk!' Royd ordered, pushing his Colt, his arm, and his head and shoulders between the curtains hanging across the room's rear window. 'Or I drop you!'

Maria screamed and flung open the bedroom door to lunge into the room and pull up short. Royd's gun swung to cover her instead. He did his sneer into leer transformation.

'Same thing but different party,' the gunman rasped.

'Jamie, everything all right in there?' Doyle called.

'Do it, Danny!' Maria implored.

Her husband hesitated for a moment. Then, as the sweat beads dried on his wan face, he released his double-handed grip on the Winchester. The rifle clattered to the floor.

'Couldn't be better, John!' Royd called, kicking loose clinging shards of glass as he swung a leg in through the broken rear window and climbed into the room. 'But I reckon it will be,' he added, his voice lower. He gestured with the gun. 'Outside, both of you! I never did get laid in the open air before.'

Danny was still standing close to where the rifle had fallen. He had been regretting the surrender from the moment he released his hold on the Winchester. Better Maria should be dead than endure what Royd planned to do to her. And yet he had let go of the rifle as a natural instinct when he saw his wife threatened with death. Now it was too late. If he made a try for the rifle, Royd would kill him: and Maria would be completely on her own.

He was utterly helpless and found it difficult to look at Maria, for he knew she would read the hopelessness he felt in his face. But he did look at her, and was momentarily confused by the expression in her eyes. Their dark irises continued to show shock and terror. But there was something else in them, too. Pleading? No. A question? No. A request? She turned slightly and reached behind her. She fastened a hand on the edge of the door and drew it closed. An odd action, which Royd was too drunk and too sexually aroused to notice.

But Danny got the message, and shot a glance through into the bedroom just before the door closed off his view. He saw the top half of the bed, with the stranger's head on the pillow. The stranger had turned his head towards the door and his eyes were open. Not much. But they were ice blue eyes which showed up clearly as glittering threads between the cracked lids. Not opened wide enough to reveal an expression. And the rest of his features were too brutalised to show anything but pain.

'I warn you . . . !' Danny started, knowing that he had only one tactic to play – to use time.

'Right friendly of you, punk!' Royd taunted. 'Never do get warned in a cat house. But I reckon I'll risk it for a piece of this Mex tail.' He aimed the Colt at a kerosene lamp on the table and squeezed off a second shot. The glass of the lamp shattered. 'Now!' he bellowed. 'Move out, both of you.'

The explosion and crash of glass almost drove Maria over the brink into hysteria. She controlled it by forcing herself to move – almost running across the room to the door. She didn't trust herself to speak, and there was no need. Danny took long strides towards her and was at her side as she stepped out onto the stoop and down onto the hard packed dirt at the side of the meadow. Royd was close behind them.

Doyle had moved his position and was standing close to the horses, barring the way to the two booted Winchesters. But that had not been his prime purpose. He had got a second bottle of whisky from Royd's saddlebag. Down on the bank of the river, the two surveyors were standing close together, staring fearfully up the slope of the meadow.

'Don't look like them city slickers is gonna to be any trouble, John,' Royd said. 'How about we try a double-up on this Mex broad?'

Danny suddenly realised there was no part he could play that would be of any use. Time had run out. Doyle had drank far into the new bottle and was wearing the same brand of leer as the shorter man. Both of them were aching for access to Maria's body and delay could only be earned by a bullet. He felt Maria insert her hand into his and this time he could not bring himself to face her. He could only stare out across the homestead land that had never been truly his. Now, the wife who had promised to be his alone was to be forced to accept other men. Forced because of his failure to protect her.

'Danny, it is my fault,' his wife said softly as the boards of the stoop creaked under Royd's weight. The gunman stepped down onto the dirt. 'I made you promise not to defend our place. Don't blame yourself, *mi bien*.'

Both of them sensed danger at the same time but only the woman started to turn. Danny had his eyes tight closed to try to hide the tears from the leering Doyle.

'No!' Maria screamed.

'Keep sayin' it, sweetheart,' Royd encouraged as he swung his Colt. The underside of the barrel and the trigger guard crashed into the side of Danny's head, just above his right ear. 'Broke in, but spirited. That's the way I like my fillies.'

The blow did not quite drive Danny Oakley into unconsciousness. But the force of it sent him staggering forward on weakened legs, tearing his hand free of his wife's grip. The horses shied away from the tottering man and Maria screamed again as Danny dropped to his knees. Maria tried to run towards him, but Royd leaned forward and shot out a curled arm. It encircled her waist and the hand cupped tight over a sparse breast.

'He didn't ought to see this, John!' Royd urged.

'Reckon not, Jamie,' Doyle agreed, stepping forward and throwing out a leg. The folded knee crashed into Danny's face and the young homesteader was pitched over backwards, stretched out flat with his legs splayed. Blood gushed from his pulped nose and his eyes snapped shut as he plunged into unconsciousness.

'That hurt, you hardnosed punk!' Doyle rasped, massaging his knee as he stepped into the inverted vee of the senseless man's spread legs. The gunman's other leg swung, and the toe of his riding boot crashed into Danny's crotch.

Maria gave out a moan as if she had herself felt the pain. It was almost masked by a harsh laugh from Doyle, who sucked from the bottle before turning to shout down the sloping meadow.

'It's okay, you guys! Survey's done! This punk's got a couple of achers!'

Royd, breathing heavily and with his arousal seeming to emanate light from his dark eyes, swung Maria around to face him and dropped his Colt. The empty hand clawed over the neckline of the worn dress and dragged downwards.

'Let's see what you got two of, sweetheart!' he rasped.

The dress ripped to the stitched waistline and the attacker spun the screaming woman around again. Now his hand hooked over the top of the back and yanked down.

'Danny!' she shrieked. 'Please. Please don't. *Por favor . . .*'

Her struggles tore her out of Royd's grip on her body. But he continued to hold the tattered bodice of the pink dress. As she plunged away from him, the stitching at the waist parted. Her arms were wrenched back and came out of the sleeves. Her torso, firm-fleshed and darkly hued, was revealed in complete nakedness as she took the first step towards escape.

Royd vented a roar of anger that suddenly became a gust of obscene laughter. The skirt section of the dress slid down over Maria's slender hips and gathered into a hobble around her ankles. With a shriek of alarm and despair, she pitched to the dirt and rolled onto the grass. Her shoes were kicked clear as she flailed her legs to get rid of the dress. But, before she could even start to rise, Royd hurled himself down on top of her.

He straddled her, sitting on her bare stomach and pinning her wrists to the ground with his hands. He ignored her crimson face stained by tears and dirt, and stared down at the light brown swells of her breasts with their large, darker coloured crests.

'Man, ain't she worth a dozen of any two dollar whore we've ever had, John?' he rasped, his voice heavy with passion.

'You know I ain't a boob man, Jamie,' Doyle answered, his voice deeper than ever. 'I got a lower opinion of females.'

'So check her out, partner. But I'll take a drink while you're at it.'

As Doyle approached, Royd released one of Maria's wrists. Her screams had ended now and low moaning sounds were issuing from her quivering lips. But then she roared a Spanish obscenity as she lashed at Royd's face with her freed hand.

'Ill tempered bitch, ain't she?' Royd said as he swung his head out of the line of the blow. Then he delivered one of his own, smashing her back-handed across the cheek and drawing blood from the corner of her mouth.

Tears of pain flowed more strongly than those of terror. Royd took the open bottle thrust at him by Doyle and tilted it to his lips. The blow had flung Maria's head to the side and seemingly had knocked all the strength and will out of her. She lay, sobbing and submissive, as the straddled man drank and his partner drew her only item of underwear down over her lithe thighs. Her eyes were closed until she felt wetness splashing down onto her exposed breasts. Then she looked up into the sweat-run face of Royd as the man tipped whisky over her upper body.

'Sometimes like to mix my liquor with a little somethin', sweetheart,' he growled at her. 'In this case, two little somethin's.' He glanced over his shoulder as he dropped the empty bottle and refastened the hand over Maria's wrist. 'What d'you see back there, John?'

The woman felt the bitterness of nausea rise into her throat as Doyle's fingers caressed and probed the intimate centre of her body.

'Dunno why they call Mexes greasers, Jamie,' came the gravel-voiced response. 'This dame's as dry as Death Valley.'

'Already whetted my appetite, partner,' Royd countered, pushing himself backwards to cover the woman's body.

His mouth, spilling the saliva of lust, opened wide. Beneath him, Maria watched in horrified fascination. But then, just as his lips fastened over one of her nipples and sucked in a painful mouthful of whisky-soaked flesh, she caught a glimpse of the unconscious Danny. She screamed – in revulsion rather than agony – and screwed her eyes tight shut. Her lips moved, forming silent words in her own language; praying for the same release into merciful unconsciousness. But the prayer went unanswered. Every act of violation upon her defenceless and naked body was too vividly experienced to be a nightmare.

Edge was watching from the bedroom and thinking coldly that the woman's suffering could be no worse than the agony he was feeling in every part of his body. He had heard every word spoken since Royd had crashed the shot from the rear window to the window at the front. Then, the moment the woman closed the door on him, he had tried to move. But bruised flesh, cracked bones and stiffened muscles refused him for a long time. And he did not succeed in sitting up and swinging his feet to the floor until the whisky pouring started. Even then, the pain blurred his vision with involuntary tears and Royd was assaulting Maria's breasts with his viciously hungry mouth when the half-breed was able to look across the room and through the lace curtains and glass to the scene of the rape.

He stood up and the groan which emerged from his throat was as involuntary as the tears. The view from the window no longer held anything for him. Royd had satisfied his mouth and was snarling in frustration as he tore at the front of his pants to free himself for the completion of the assault. Doyle was standing over the couple, face dark with impatient lust. The horses had backed away, as if in distaste at what was happening. Finbar and Standish had closed in. Both surveyors expressed excitement at what they were witnessing. Danny Oakley was still sprawled where he had fallen, inert except for the shallow motion of his chest as he breathed.

Edge caught sight of himself in a mirror standing on a bureau and leaning against the wall. He saw the taping around his rib cage, the crusting of dried salve on several areas of his chest, and the mass of bruises and cuts on his face.

'If you were a horse, they'd have shot you,' he told himself.

There was a shrill scream from outside, as Royd finally penetrated deep and hard into the bride of three weeks.

'First time I've had to bore my own well!' the rapist yelled gleefully.

The noise did not draw Edge's hooded eyes in their bruised surrounds away from his reflection. The pain had stopped hitting him in waves and become a constant force. It tried to urge him back onto the luxury of the waiting bed. Instead, he took a slow, tentative step towards the door, easing his eyes open wider to clear them of the haze which was part of pain's attack. He thought about the vague recollections he had of the couple he had seen, upside-down beneath the belly of the horse. And about the degree of pain he had been suffering then. A lot worse than it was now: and it was the Mexican woman and the freckle-faced feller who had made it easier. Had patched him up and put him into bed.

He recalled, too, thinking how he had wanted no favours. But circumstances had insisted he accept them. He reached the door and opened it. The yells of the gunmen were louder now, coming in through the open door at the front of the house and the smashed window.

Sunlight sparkled on glass from the window and the shattered lamp. It dazzled Edge and then made the room dark as an after-effect. He screwed his eyes shut and the skin around them smarted.

The woman had come into the bedroom when trouble started and asked for help. Edge could give it now and be out of debt to the couple. He found he could not raise his arm high enough to reach for the razor. The flesh at the nape of his neck refused to acknowledge, even, that the razor was in its accustomed place. He opened his eyes, not looking at the glass, and sought his gear. It wasn't in the room. The Winchester Danny Oakley had surrendered was still were he dropped it.

Edge moved to where it lay, glass crunching under his feet. They had not taken off his boots and he wondered fleetingly if the couple had expected him to die. He stooped, snatched at the rifle and straightened. The whole world spun crazily and the room darkened again. A dry retch emerged from his throat. The lace curtains seemed like an impenetrable barrier across the smashed window. He moved to the door.

'Me and John share everything, sweetheart!' Royd yelled. 'Ain't that right, John?'

'On the whole!' Doyle rasped. A loud sigh of relief signalled his entry into the woman. She made no sound.

'Okay, John?'

'Terrific, Jamie!'

Edge had been in the middle of a rambling dream about his long dead brother when the calling of the familiar name catapulted him back to awareness. Now he stepped into the doorway and saw clearly the man whose name it was and the man who had called to him.

Doyle, his pants down around his kneels to expose his quivering rump, was on top of the broken Maria and thrusting into her. Royd was watching eagerly as he refastened the front of his pants. The two surveyors were still where Edge had first seen them. Finbar had a hand down the front of his pants and was breathing heavily in a pleasure that was only partly vicarious. Standish looked on the point of throwing up. He was gazing everywhere except at the new rapist and his victim. And his revolted gaze at last fastened on the tall apparition-like form of Edge as the half-breed emerged from the house onto the stoop.

'Oh!' he gasped, and the monosyllable triggered his nausea. A stream of multi-coloured vomit gushed from his mouth and he dropped to his knees and hung his head.

He was totally ignored by the sexually aroused Doyle and Finbar and the sex-satiated Royd.

'I sure greased her for you, John!' Royd yelled.

'Looks to me like the lady don't want servicing,' Edge growled. To his own ears his voice sounded the way it did when it first broke in his youth. But it had the power and volume to cut across the retching of Standish and grunts and heavy breathing of the rapist and his audience.

The Winchester was aimed at Doyle as all eyes except those of the unconscious Oakley and his violated wife swung to stare at Edge. It was a difficult shot because of the man's intimate closeness to Maria. But it had to be the first one, because Doyle was still wearing his sixgun and he reached down his body for it. And Doyle realised his advantage. As he drew the Colt from the holster, he rolled off the naked woman in an effort to put himself behind her. His exposed genitals provided an obscene and appropriate target. But the half-breed had already elected to go for a head shot and he moved the Winchester only a fraction of an inch to take account of Doyle's roll. The gunman had his hand fisted around the butt of the Colt when he died. The rifle shell smashed into the side of his head, angled up through the brain and exploded clear in a welter of bone splinters and blood at the crown of his skull.

Maria continued to lay inert and silent as gore from the entry wound splashed onto her terror-stricken face.

'I did nothing!' Finbar shrieked as Edge leaned back against the door jamb and swung the Winchester.

The recoil of the rifle shot had produced a fresh attack of intense agony as its jarring effect was transmitted to every part of Edge's punished body. But survival was still the name of the game and he used every ounce of his will power to fight back the wave of crimson that threatened to blind him. His eyes and the Winchester muzzle whipped past the man in the city suit and located the gunman without a gun. Royd was trying to regain the Colt he had discarded earlier. He hit the ground at the end of a dive and his fingertips curled over the butt of the gun.

Edge's vision was blurred, but the crimson had receded. He was looking through stinging beads of sweat which had run down his forehead and dripped from his eyebrows. He squeezed the trigger. The shot was short, burrowing into the grass as Royd got a firm grip on his gun, rolled, sat up and took aim. Two gunshots sounded, almost as one. The sharper crack was fractionally ahead and the Winchester's recoil was too much for the half-breed this time. It turned his body, twisting him in through the doorway and knocking him to the floor. Royd's bullet chipped wood splinters from the door frame where, an instant before, Edge's chest had been in line. Royd had no time for a second shot. His life had run out, leaving his body on the initial blood rush from the gaping holes at each side of his neck.

'Please!' Finbar shrieked, staring at the open doorway through which Edge had been thrown. 'Standish and I did nothing.'

His hand was out from the front of his pants now and both hands were held out far in front of him, palms opened in a gesture of innocence.

'That's just it,' Standish groaned as he climbed weakly to his feet, his stomach emptied of sickness. 'We stood and watched and did nothing. We deserve what ... '

His voice dried up as Edge staggered into the doorway again, the blue slits in the punished flesh of his face raking over the scene of sudden death and violence on the meadow before the house. He was still holding the rifle, but now it provided a crutch to support him on one side while he leaned his shoulder against the door jamb.

'Relax, feller,' he said evenly and his voice sounded better now. But the weakness and pain warned him he was a long way from recovered in other directions. 'One good turn don't deserve more than two others.'

Maria Oakley got slowly to her feet as Edge talked and held the apprehensive attention of the two surveyors. Then she suddenly lunged into fast movement. She raced to where the wreckage of her dress lay, snatched it up and held it against the front of her body as she went to her husband's side and squatted. Despite the tattered dress, there was a lot of her firm, dark-hued body still displayed. But none of the men looked at anything except her face as she raised her head after checking her unconscious husband. Relief showed through the anguish as the woman's dark eyes swept from Edge to the surveyors and back again.

'He's going to be all right,' she pronounced with conviction.

'And you, madam?' Standish asked, his posture one of stiff attention. 'You will be all right, too? After what you were forced to go through?'

Maria's pretty features formed into a grimace as she glanced at the bodies of Doyle and Royd slumped across patches of congealed blood. If she was aware that spots of Doyle's blood blemished her face, it did not bother her. 'It is wrong what is said,' she murmured. 'Such a fate is not worse than death.'

'Is there anything we can do to help?' Standish offered. His partner seemed too terrified to speak.

'Just go!' Maria replied, her tone abruptly hard. 'Get off this property.'

Finbar found his voice at last. 'Mr Ryan has hired us to do a survey, Mrs Oakley,' he said, a little pompously. 'I really think we should – '

Maria moved quickly again – and abandoned modesty. When she lunged to the side and scooped up Royd's Colt, she could only retain one hand hold on the tattered dress. Her movements swung the material to reveal tantalising glimpses of her body. But again, nobody looked at the woman's most intimate parts. This time, attention switched from her face to the gun and back again.

'If he won't kill you, I will!' she snapped, with a toss of her head to indicate Edge. 'Unless you get on your horses and ride off this property.'

'Quite so, madam,' Standish said, and wasted no time in mounting his mare.

Finbar got into the saddle with greater reluctance. 'Mr Ryan will be most annoyed,' he said. 'Really we should complete our work here.'

'You saw what happened to him, feller,' Edge muttered, nodding his aching head towards Doyle, whose unfeeling genitals were still exposed to view.

Standish nodded. 'We saw what happened to both of them, sir.'

'But he's the one to get the message from,' the half-breed supplemented. 'So best you ride, uh? He died on the job.'

Chapter Six

THE longer Edge had stayed in the doorway, the stronger he felt. Compared, that was, to the brink of collapse he had been at when he first rose from the bed. After he had watched the two surveyors ride from sight where the trail turned between the trees and the river bank, he was able to do away with the rifle as a crutch and stand erect without the support of the door jamb.

'Thank you,' Maria said suddenly, to break the silence which had followed after the hoofbeats faded from earshot. 'You owed us no debt, but I am grateful you felt that you did.'

She had not idly watched the surveyors ride off the homestead. While the half-breed's eyes were averted, she had worked nimbly with the remains of the dress. When he looked at her now, he saw that she had fashioned a halter to conceal her breasts, and a short skirt to cover her from waist to just above her knees. Had the circumstances been different, he might have found this attire more stimulating than her former nudity. The words had drawn Edge's attention back to her and he watched the woman as she stooped and gathered up the limp form of her husband in her arms.

'You owe us nothing now, that is certain,' she said as she approached the doorway. 'And I need the bed for Danny.'

Edge nodded and stepped out of her path. Her only sign of strain was the heavy sheen of sweat coating her blood-spotted face. 'Glad you see it that way, ma'am. If you'll tell me where my stuff is, I'll be moving on.'

'Danny put everything in the barn,' Maria called from inside the barn. 'Your clothes, too. I am a clean housekeeper for my husband.' The door started to close. 'No offence.' It closed.

Oakley was not the only one to benefit from Maria's belief in cleanliness. The first things Edge saw when he entered the barn were his shirt and undershirt hung and dried after being laundered.

The feeling of returned strength was proved to be false as he undertook the simple task of dressing. The bulkiness of the bandages made the familiar clothing a tight fit, but Edge seldom lied to others and never lied to himself. He could manage a short, slow walk in the noonday sun without trouble. Anything more than this required a major effort from his tortured body.

But his honesty was matched by his determination. It took him thirty sweating, grunting, cursing minutes to saddle the big gelding Woodrow Ryan had provided for him. But he did it, and a sense of grim satisfaction was not all he got out of the exercise. He was rested and he was patched up. Use of his muscles took the stiffness out of his limbs. Thus, as he buckled on his gunbelt and checked the Colt, then the Winchester, his actions were smoother and more agile. Then he looked in the saddlebags and abruptly reached the fullest extent of recovery that was humanly possible so soon after the beating.

The horse had not been his last night. But the saddle and other gear that was carried along with the senseless rider to the Oakley homestead had always been the half-breed's. So Ryan's hands had taken the trouble to let him keep what belonged to him – with a single exception. A stack of bills totalling more than three thousand dollars was missing.

After he had completed a second search of both saddlebags, the tall half-breed sensed even more strength surge through his lean frame. But he had been fooled again. When he tried to mount, he fell back hard to the straw-covered floor of the rich-smelling stable and almost stumbled over onto his rump. The dark eyes of the black and white gelding gazed at the man with disdain.

'We all have our off days,' Edge growled, showing the animal a grim frown, then taking more care with his second attempt to mount.

He got astride the big horse this time and sat there, unmoving and allowing the world to get back onto an even keel. He knew what had happened: he had confused will power with the physical kind. Already firmly resolved to avenge the beating he had been given, that determination had been manifoldly strengthened when he discovered his bankroll gone. But his body could not yet deliver what his mind demanded. And that could be a dangerous fault when he met up with the Ryan hands he intended to find.

But time would pass before that happened.

'You're not strong enough to ride yet, mister,' Danny Oakley called as Edge eased his horse out of the stable.

The half-breed had been blind and deaf to everything but his own actions and feelings since making it to the stable from the house. Now he saw that he was not the only beaten man to be back on his feet and painfully active. The young homesteader, the crown of his head heavily patched with a wad of white dressing, was in the process of tying the body of Jamie Royd to the dead man's horse. Doyle was already lashed across his own saddle.

Oakley's freckles were more prominent than ever against the paleness of his skin. And he winced each time he moved his bandaged head.

'I am sorry I told you to leave. I did not mean to say such a thing. I was upset by what happened.'

Maria was standing on the stoop. She was modestly dressed now, in what was probably her Sunday best. A gown of white satin trimmed with blue lace at the arms, neckline and hem. Her pretty face was washed clean of blood and dirt. Her hands trembled only slightly as they held a tray on which were three cups of steaming coffee. She started and coffee slopped over the rims when her husband yelled and delivered two open-handed blows to the rumps of the horses burdened with dead men. The animals snorted and plunged into a gallop, scattering sheep and frightening the milk cow as they angled across the meadow to the trail where it went from sight around the timber stand.

'But I guess you're set on leavin',' Danny allowed with a sigh. 'Be happy, though, if you'd share some coffee with us. Maybe a bite to eat if you've got an appetite.'

Edge turned the gelding to head him towards the front of the house as Oakley made for the same destination. The homesteader made it first and took a cup from the tray. Maria picked up her coffee and extended the tray towards Edge. The half-breed accepted the drink with a grim-faced nod, noting that he was honoured with the only cup that was not chipped and cracked.

'Got no appetite for food,' he said, blowing on the surface of the steaming, dark black liquid and relishing the aroma that rose with the vapour. He drew his Colt without haste and rested his wrist on the saddle-horn as he cocked the hammer and aimed the gun at Maria. Neither his expression nor his tone changed. 'But I'm real hungry to get back the money that was stole from me.'

Maria gasped and took a backward step. She started to turn. Edge, his movements almost lazy, swivelled the Colt, squeezed the trigger, and cocked it again as he returned to cover his original target. Maria's index finger was still hooked through the handle of the cup. The rest of the crock was in a hundred pieces, flying across the stoop in a deluge of scalding hot coffee.

'Be obliged you stayed where you are, ma'am,' the half-breed said softly. 'If you want, you can pray I'm going to believe what your husband tells me.'

Edge concentrated his attention on the woman. But he could see the shadow of Danny Oakley. When the shadow moved, the half-breed sighed. Then:

'Don't be crazy, feller! Me and the lady already agreed we don't owe each other a thing. I'll kill her as easy as you butcher a sheep when you need the meat.' His thin lips curled back and the twinge of pain he experienced made the smile colder than ever. 'And one man's meat is another man's money.'

The shadow of Danny became as unmoving as the slender body of his wife. His voice sounded a sliver away from cracking and the half-breed's glittering blue eyes expressed grim satisfaction. The Oakleys were near the ends of their tethers and all the fight had been drained out of them.

'I don't know what you're talkin' about, mister! Me and Maria didn't touch nothin' of yours 'ceptin' to get to where you was hurt and to tend to your horse.'

'Three thousand dollars, give or take a few,' Edge insisted.

'We are not thieves!' Maria snapped, showing a little spirit. But she held her frozen posture.

'You can search every square inch of the farm,' Danny offered.

'Ain't got energy for that feller. Nor the time.'

'Where was the money?' Maria asked, a little desperately.

'Saddlebags.'

'In the barn,' the woman said with a vigorous nod of her head. 'The two men who . . . who you killed. They went into the barn for awhile. The others as well, maybe. I am not sure.'

'No, not the surveyors,' Danny said definitely. 'Not before I was hit on the head, anyway.' He shrugged. 'And Royd and Doyle did not go beyond the doorway. I was watchin' them.'

'Are you sure you had the money after the men who beat you tied you to the horse?' the woman asked. She turned now, to face Edge squarely. Fear had gone from her dark eyes and she gave the impression of being intently anxious to help. Somehow, the fact that her life depended upon the whereabouts of the missing money seemed unimportant to her.

Edge looked away from her and met the steady gaze of Danny. The freckled-faced youngster wore a look that was something akin to disgust. The half-breed gave a slight nod and slid the Colt into its holster. Both the Oakleys waited for him to say something, but he merely sipped at his coffee and glanced over his shoulder to where the surveyors and the dead gunmen had gone from sight.

'You're goin' to try to get your money back?' Danny asked at length.

Edge shook his head. 'Gonna do better than try, feller.' He shrugged. 'Or maybe worse. I'm gonna get it back or I'm gonna die.'

The coffee tasted as good as it smelled. He thought it had probably scalded his throat, but he had very little feeling there. He rolled a cigarette one-handed as he finished drinking, then extended the empty cup towards Maria. The liquid swilling around in his empty stomach reminded him that it was a long time since he had eaten. When he sucked the acrid tobacco smoke deep inside him it emphasised his need for food. But he didn't want anything more from these people.

'We heard about the three men who tried to hire you,' Oakley said. His voice seemed to come from a long way off. Yet the young homesteader was standing less than a dozen feet from where Edge sat astride the gelding. 'Seems they had to die afore they got what they wanted.'

Edge shook his head and his vision blurred. But the distortion was caused neither by tears of pain nor the sweat of exertion. 'I'm going back up the valley on my own business, feller.'

He wheeled the gelding slowly, and felt himself sway in the saddle. He had to press his feet hard against the stirrups to right himself.

'You go against Ryan and his men and that's everybody's business in this valley!' Danny Oakley called.

His voice was coming from an immense distance away now. And it had an echo that repeated the words and added a shriller note. Yet Edge had moved the gelding no more than a few paces. The sun on the river turned the water to a dazzling silver that caused the half-breed to crack his eyes almost closed. The trees were swaying this way and that. Yet the heat remained as high as ever, with not a breath of cooling air.

'I've gotta be crazy,' he muttered, and saw the gelding's ears prick to the sound of his voice.

'Please stay a while longer!' Maria called from behind him. She sounded a lot closer than her husband had. 'It's not safe to ride out like that.'

Astride the gelding which moved at an easy walk, will power could compensate for lack of physical strength. Edge ignored the tricks which his punchdrunk mind was playing on him and recalled every lesson he had ever learned about survival. He thought about the pain of the beating. About the humiliation of being helpless in front of witnesses while the three men lashed at him with fists and booted feet. He started to count dollar bills, aiming to reach three thousand.

But the sparkling river continued to dazzle him and the trees didn't stop swaying. The heat rose and he could feel his clothing sticking to his flesh by sweat. He trusted the Oakleys not to cause him harm, despite his dumb move of accusing them of theft and threatening the woman. But the Oakley farm was the scene of a setback for Woodrow Ryan. Ryan would not let it pass without extracting retribution of some kind. So Ryan men would return to the Oakley place: and the young couple were no match for the kind of backing the rich rancher could command.

To be found on the place by Ryan men would be no picnic for Edge. To be found there unconscious . . .

The half-breed was halfway across the meadow. The sheep looked at him from one side and the milk cow watched him from the other. All the animals were chewing rhythmically on mouthfuls of the lush grass. He was too far away from where the Oakleys stood to hear what they said to each other.

'I put something in his coffee, Danny,' Maria revealed.

'You did what?'

'You need time, Danny.'

He thought about this, then he nodded. 'I guess I can try.' He stared out down the sloping meadow to where Edge was sagging in the saddle and swaying like a drunken man. 'What did you use?'

'The powder the animal doctor gave us for when the cow calves. The cow never goes right to sleep. So I gave the stranger twice the amount.'

'Good God, Maria!' Danny exclaimed. 'It could kill him!'

He stared at his wife and saw an expression which he had never before seen on her pretty face. Grim resolution which was completely lacking in compassion. A feminine variation of the look which he had seen on the battered face of the half-breed. The lines into which her features were formed seemed to add ten years to her age.

'To us it makes no difference, Danny,' she said heavily. 'Gone from here or dead it is the same. He serves no purpose.'

'I've never seen you like this before, Maria!' the man rasped.

'I've never been like this before, Danny,' his wife answered.

Both stared down the meadow as the half-breed finally swayed too far to one side and toppled out of the saddle.

'What a time to drop out,' he muttered, or thought, just before he thudded to the grass and plunged into unconsciousness again.

Chapter Seven

IT was night when he came out of it and his return to awareness was better than the last time. The pains did not spring from so many parts of his body and there was less sharpness to them. Total recall was slower in coming to a mind that felt dazed in a head which seemed to be twice as large and four times as heavy as usual. Edge had experienced two massive drinking jags in his life. Once during the war and again after the brutal death of his wife. Now as he raised himself to his feet in the bedroom of the Oakley house his feelings were identical to the hangovers he had gone through in the distant past.

But he had no reason to suspect he had been drugged. He put down the second period of unconsciousness to the same cause as the first: and he was grateful for it. He had needed the rest and in this respect the cause which had forced it upon him was immaterial. The renewed strength he felt as he crossed to the door and opened it was no trick. The aroma of cooked food that came to him stimulated his gastric juices and he felt capable of eating everything in the house.

The main room was neat and tidy again, with the drape curtains drawn across the broken windows to keep in the light of the lamp. The glass from the windows and the old lamp had been swept up and all the crude furniture was in its correct place. There was a square of white linen on the table and Danny and Maria Oakley were eating stew. A third chair was drawn up to the table, before a place setting. The couple were as neat and clean as their surroundings.

'You are feeling better?' Maria asked.

'You look better, mister,' Danny added.

'Then I look the way I feel,' the half-breed answered as the woman gestured for him to take the vacant place at the table. 'No more callers?'

As he sat down, Maria ladled out a portion of the meaty stew onto his plate.

'We're better than a day's hard ride from Greenville,' Danny answered. 'And the Big R ranch-house is fifteen miles north of town.'

Maria cooked as well as she did most other things around the house. Edge's ravenous hunger caused him to swallow the first few mouthfuls without bothering to taste the food. But then he slowed down. He stopped eating suddenly.

'I can't pay for the food right now,' he said.

'Don't insult us in our own house,' Maria answered grimly.

'You've made your point, mister!' Danny said earnestly. 'You don't take nothin' for nothin'. So, by your rules, we're even on everythin' else.'

Edge resumed eating. 'I'll listen to a deal, feller,' he offered. 'But I ain't leading no army of downtrodden dirt farmers against the Big R.'

'It isn't because you're afraid, I know this,' Maria said.

'Then you ain't so smart as you think you are,' the half-breed told her. 'The reason I turned down those three fellers back up the valley was because they scared the hell out of me.'

Both the Oakleys expressed puzzlement.

'I survived a war that went on better than five years,' he augmented. 'And the way I did it was by making professional soldiers out of the men assigned to me. They knew what to do, how to do it and when to do it. A lot of times without me having to open my mouth. Every one of them was either a born killer or had a natural bent for killing.'

He finished the plate of stew and waved away Maria's offer of a second helping. He took out the makings and began to roll the paper around the tobacco.

'It figures Ryan has some men like that. Not all of them, but some. And some is enough.' He lit the cigarette and pushed his chair back from the table to stand up. 'If I have to go up against them to get my money back, I'll feel a hell of a lot safer knowing I only have me to rely on. But with a whole bunch of farmers carrying a load of resentment as well as guns they've never fired to kill before . . . well, I just never did have an ambition to die in Texas.' He showed a quiet grin. 'It's too close to hell.'

He saw his hat hanging on one of a line of pegs on the wall beside the door. He put it on and looked back at the couple sitting on either side of the table. Maria was looking faintly amused.

'For a man like you, I think that is a very long speech, *senor*,' she said quietly.

He nodded. 'But I figure I got breath enough left to get where I'm going.'

Danny stood up. 'Would you object to company?' He licked his lips. 'That was what I intended to ask for if you insisted upon repaying us for the meal – to ride north with you.'

'You scared of the dark, feller?'

Danny seemed on the point of blowing up into anger, but his more controlled wife cleared her throat loudly and the tension drained out of him. 'I want to talk to Ryan,' he said evenly. 'Like I told you, he lives a long way from here. But his hands ride all over the valley. It could be those two surveyors ran into some gunmen and told them what happened here. And the gunmen could take it into their heads to do somethin' without waitin' to get the word from their boss.' He shook his head. 'It ain't the dark I'm scared of, mister.'

'And her?' Edge asked, stabbing a finger towards Maria.

'My wife will ride into El Paso and stay at the hotel until I come to fetch her.'

The half-breed pursed his thin lips and thought about the proposition for a few moments. Then he nodded. 'Keep the goodbyes short, feller. Longer I'm without my bankroll, more chance it has of being smaller when I get it back.'

As he pulled open the door and stepped out into the cool night, Maria got to her feet and Danny moved around the table, arms stretching out for an embrace. They had unsaddled his horse again and, this time, it was a lot easier to get him ready for riding. The horses from the corral had been led into shelter for the night and, because the moonlight shafting in through the open doorway did not reach the stalls, the half-breed failed to notice that one of the animals was still wet with the sweat of a hard ride.

Oakley came into the stable as Edge led the black and white gelding outside. Maria stood in the open doorway of the house, her slender figure silhouetted against the rectangle of lamplight behind her. The half-breed swung into the saddle and held his horse to a walk as he approached the house.

He touched the brim of his hat. 'Obliged for everything you did, ma'am,' he told her softly. 'And I hope everything works out for you here in the valley.'

'We will just have to wait and see,' she replied. 'But you do not really care, I think?'

'Just passing the time of day.'

'It is night, *senor*. And you are like the night. You come and you go. Sometimes without trouble. Often with a storm. You ask for nothing and you make no apology for anything you do.'

'And you're a day person, ma'am?'

'There are few who do not like the day better than the night.'

'Guess I can't argue with that,' Edge told her, turning his horse in a slow wheel.

'But you will take care of Danny for as long as he is with you? He is not a man of the gun.'

'Go to El Paso, Mrs Oakley,' the half-breed told her. 'And worry about him. That's all you can do.'

'But you can do more,' she insisted. 'If you want.'

'You know what I want,' he called over his shoulder, and heeled his horse towards the trail as Oakley led a tan mare from the stables and swung up into the saddle. The young home-steader had the Winchester slid into the boot and he was wearing a gunbelt with the holster attached high on his right hip.

'You are a hard man to like, *senor*!' Maria called as she watched her husband close with Edge and match the jogging pace across the meadow.

Danny Oakley frowned at the battered profile of Edge's face as he drew level with the half-breed. 'Don't think badly of Maria, mister,' he said. 'She's not herself today. What with almost gettin' raped by those two gunslingers.'

Edge avoided looking at his riding companion. Instead, he glanced back over his shoulder and caught a final glimpse of the silhouetted form in the house doorway before the trees intervened. What Oakley had said explained the strange con-versation of a few moments ago. Maria had intended to warn Edge that she had lied to her husband about the assaults on her. But the half-breed had moved away before the woman could talk herself into making the admission.

'Your wife's all right, Oakley,' Edge said, and curled back his lips to show a grin. The skin of his face did not hurt quite so much anymore when he altered the set of his expression. 'But then Mexican women usually are.'

'Maria reckoned as how she thought you had some Mexican in you someplace, mister,' Oakley answered.

'My Pa was from Mexico. Which gives you and me something in common, I figure.'

'How's that?' Oakley asked, confused.

Edge showed more of his teeth to brighten the grin. 'We both got Mex better halves, feller.'

Chapter Eight

MIDNIGHT came and went and the weather remained pleasantly cool under a bright, clear sky. The two riders were on the main trail by then, having swung by the Clayton property and two other homesteads. All three houses and their immediate surroundings were basically similar to the Oakley place: small, but neat and tidy and well tended. At such an hour there were no lights burning, and the sound of hoofbeats nearby did not spur the tenant farmers to fire lamps and check on the riders. There were no sounds of alarm from disturbed stock.

Edge and Oakley did not talk as they rode, even though the easy pace which the half-breed set would have made conversation unstrained. The varying speed between a trot and a canter had a twofold reason – to conserve the strength of the horses and to ease the pain which the ride was reawakening within Edge.

But the half-breed showed no signs of distress as he rode erect in the saddle, constantly swinging his head this way and that – surveying the valley to his left, his right and behind him as well as up ahead. Danny Oakley was equally as watchful, but his attitude was tense and rigid: his posture as stiff as the anxious lines of his freckled face.

Paradoxically, when galloping hoofbeats sounded on the trail behind them and men's voices were raised to shout, some of the tension went out of the young homesteader. Edge was aware of this as he reined the gelding to a halt and rested a hand loosely around the stock of the booted Winchester.

'It's okay, mister!' Oakley said quickly, peering intently back along the trail, the hard-packed stretch of sun-baked dirt standing out white against the dark expanses of grassland spread on either side. 'Looks like Jack Clayton and Dale Anson.'

Edge's glittering eyes moved away from Oakley to stare down the trail. All he could make out of the riders were two patches of dark shadow against the paler colour of dust rising from beneath the pumping hooves of their mounts. He spat. 'With eyesight good as you got, Oakley, you just got to have a daughter you'll call Annie.'

The youngster's relief became more expansive. He grinned happily at the half-breed. 'Maria just plans for a boy, mister. Gonna call him after me.'

'Little Danny Oakley,' Edge mused pensively as the two newcomers neared, slowing their horses. 'Don't really have a musical ring to it.'

'Thought that was you, Oakley,' the skinny, middle-aged Clayton said. 'Was over at Anson's place and we saw you ride by. Mind if we stick with you? Headin' for Greenville.'

Clayton and Anson both eyed Edge apprehensively. Anson was a few years older than the thin man. He was a paunchy, moon-faced man with wire-framed spectacles perched on his snub nose. One of the side pieces was missing but the glasses seemed firmly set. Both men carried sixguns in their holsters and had rifles in their saddleboots.

'This here is . . . Hey, I never did get to know your name, mister.' Oakley was the happiest Edge had seen him on a day when he had seen little and all of it bad.

'Edge.'

Oakley blinked. 'Just Edge?'

'Been enough for me for a long time.'

'You mind if my neighbours ride with us?'

Edge spat again. 'It's an open trail. But I ain't in such an all-fire hurry as they were just now.'

'Just tryin' to catch you is all, Mr Edge,' Anson said. He had a high-pitched nervous sounding voice.

'I been caught,' Edge allowed, fixing Oakley with a hard, penetrating stare. 'But you ain't got a hook sunk into me.'

He clucked to the gelding and tapped lightly with his heels. He held the animal on a loose rein and the trio of farmers fell in

6

behind him. If there was talk between the three, Edge did not hear it. But it probably wasn't necessary, anyway. Tacit questions asked with inquiring looks could be answered by a nod or shake of the head. Oakley would only have had to ride to his nearest neighbour. That neighbour – Clayton or Anson? – would have agreed to pass the word on along the valley. And, even if somebody disagreed with the plan, there would have been no harm in carrying the message.

Then Edge cleared his mind of such a line of thought, for it could lead to a futile anger and there was a more important problem confronting him – the even chance possibility that Ryan men were already looking for him after hearing from the two surveyors. That any rise of ground, pile of boulders, dip or stand of timber could conceal a bunch of men eager to fulfil Ryan's threat. *If you show your battered features here again, you'll be killed on sight.* Edge raised a hand and his exploring fingers traced the bruises and lacerations marking the flesh of his face. *Fair warnin' from a fair man.* The half-breed smiled grimly to himself. The way he looked now, maybe Ryan's men wouldn't recognise him on sight.

Edge halted his horse abruptly and the gelding vented a low whinny at the sudden interruption of the easy trek. 'Greenville's gonna be real busy come morning. If they're some more of your neighbours,' he said softly, without turning around.

The trail had been rising up a gentle slope, cutting between tall trees. The timber gave out at the crest of the incline and the downward slope was steeper and covered with low brush. Below, a narrow stream meandered from west to east, its shallow water trickling over rocks to join the main river of the valley which was hidden by intervening high ground. Some seven men had dismounted at the point where the trail forded the stream. Most of them were smoking as their horses sucked from the stream. They were about a half mile away from where the three farmers inched their mounts forward to join Edge at his vantage point.

'My eyes ain't what they used to be,' Clayton said nervously.

'And mine sure ain't,' Anson added, low but strangely shrill.

Oakley stared hard down the slope, but shook his head. 'I ain't been livin' in the valley long enough to know too many folks.'

Had there been nothing abnormal about one of the men,

Edge would have been unable to do more than hazard a guess about the group, for they were merely shadowy forms against the moon-silvered stream water. And he didn't notice that one of the seven was bigger than all the others until the giant flicked away his cigarette and unfolded himself from the rock upon which he had been sitting. Then the half-breed massaged each of his upper arms in turn, unaware which of the two giants it was down at the stream.

If there was talk among the men at the ford, it was not loud enough to carry up the slope to the four on the crest of the rise. But the clop of hooves sounded as the six horses were mounted and rode up the start of the hill at an easy walk.

'But I don't like it, Mr Edge,' Oakley muttered, as anxious as his fellow farmers. 'They're comin' the wrong way.'

'And they made a big mistake,' the half-breed said softly, swinging from the saddle and taking up the reins of the gelding to lead the animal off the trail and into the trees.

The farmers were quick to follow his actions and they needed no warning to be quiet.

'You recognise them?' Oakley asked as the horses were being hitched to trees some twenty feet back from the trail and hidden from it by the intervening trunks.

'I got some painful memories of one them,' the half-breed allowed, sliding the Winchester from his saddle boot. He pumped the action.

Oakley, Clayton and Anson slid out their rifles. Two Winchesters and an old Henry repeater.

'Thought you fellers had business in town?' Edge asked.

The freckle-faced youngster managed to grin while his neighbours continued to express apprehension.

'If you were a fool, Edge, I wouldn't be here. And I wouldn't have talked these men into joining us. Our business is wherever Ryan's hands get in our way.'

Because they were back from the crest, the rise of land acted as a sound barrier against the clop of approaching hooves. But all four men in the trees knew that open country could play tricks with acoustics. So their voices were low.

'You're lucky I can think straighter now, feller,' Edge told Oakley. 'If my brain was still addled I might not have remembered you did your Paul Revere's ride stunt before I told you what I think about fighting with amateurs.'

The youngster tried to match the grimness of expression Edge showed. But he didn't have such a long experience of hardship and suffering to call upon. All he had was determination and enthusiasm.

'Amateur fighters, maybe!' he rasped. 'But professional farmers, mister. And Ryan's tryin' to take our livelihoods away from us. He's got a map now. As well as the claim papers. That's what the surveyors are all about.'

'Yeah!' Anson cut in, and the talk was giving him some spirit. 'I talked with one of them city fellers. Seems Ryan figures to put up fences around our property. And stop right-of-way across the open range he says is his. If we're on our land when the fences go up, we won't be able to get off. And if we're off it, we won't –'

'So you got no reason to doubt we don't mean business, mister!' Clayton growled, pumping the action of his Henry. 'We're fightin' for somethin' closer to home than whether the White House is in Washington or Richmond. Get me?'

Edge pursed his lips and raked his hard-eyed gaze around the grim-set faces of the ill-matched men. 'Looks like I got you,' he allowed.

'So what you gonna do with us?' Anson asked, a note of urgency in his voice now that the clop of hooves against the hard trail could be heard.

The half-breed jerked a thumb in the direction from which the horsemen were approaching. 'One of these fellers stands near seven feet tall. Too big to miss. I want you to miss him.'

'And the others?' Clayton asked, caressing the stock of his Henry as though it was a woman's thigh – a woman other than his wife.

'That's your business,' Edge said, and moved quickly away from the group, heading on a diagonal line back towards the trail.

Oakley made to follow him, but Clayton laid a restraining hand on his arm. 'What we gonna do?' he wanted to know.

Oakley swallowed hard and Anson took advantage of the pause.

'We gonna kill 'em?'

The younger man looked into the faces of the two older ones and saw the mixture of fear and horror in their expressions. 'We do what we have to do!' he rasped, dragged himself clear of Clayton's grasp and moved directly back to the trail.

Edge was in a position to see the riders before they reached the top of the slope from the stream. He lay prone in the brush just beyond the trees. He had taken off his hat and peered over its brim – so that just his eyes and that part of his forehead beneath his dark hair provided tell-tale areas of lightness against the dark backdrop of his cover. But the men astride the horses were unsuspicious of their surroundings. They rode in attitudes of relaxed weariness, two men talking quietly together while a third was whistling tunelessly.

The big man – closer to six feet six than seven feet – rode at the centre of the group. This fact erupted a grimace across the half-breed's hidden face. But that was all. If the farmers panicked and started to blast wildly, there was a good chance the giant would take a fatal bullet. Edge accepted the possibility and resigned himself to it. Then, when the back-marker of the group reached the top of the slope and rode into the trees, Edge put his hat back on his head and crept forward.

'What the hell?' a man demanded gruffly.

Horses were brought to a halt.

'You're Jack Clayton! Seen you in Greenville!'

'Right enough!' Clayton acknowledged. 'Drop your guns, you men. And get down off your horses.'

From the side of the trail, Edge could see into the trees. He couldn't see Clayton, but it was obvious where the farmer was: for all the mounted men were staring directly ahead. Clayton had simply stepped out on to the trail, and aimed the Henry to back up his demand for surrender.

'You just gotta be kiddin'!' somebody said in an incredulous tone. 'Toss away that iron, grandpa – and we won't say nothin' of this to Mr Ryan.'

'What when we do like you say, oldtimer?' somebody else asked.

Edge was trying to recognise voices: endeavouring to match them with those he had heard before pain had distorted them. But he failed. Among this group, the only man who mattered to him was the giant.

'You won't come to no harm,' Clayton promised. 'Held prisoner until we done what we fix to do.'

'We?'

'Me,' Dale Anson put in.

'And me and some others,' Danny Oakley added.

The mounted men craned their necks to look upwards. First into the foliage on the left of the trail, then the right.

'High climbers, ain't they?' a Ryan man growled.

The half-breed grinned to himself. For amateurs, the farmers were doing fine. So far they had made only one mistake – they had called the Ryan men instead of blasting at them without warning. Then they got a warning.

'Listen, you crazy sodbusters! The only guys we want are Oakley and that beat-up Edge drifter.' The speaker was at the front of the group and he looked up into the trees on the right again. 'That's you up there, ain't it, Oakley?'

'Do like Jack Clayton told you!' the young homesteader rasped.

'Give yourself up, kid!' the Ryan man countered. 'Mr Ryan wants to talk to you, is all. It's the drifter he really has the grudge against. You give yourself up and neither you nor these two others gets hurt.' His tone became more menacing. 'Nor that wife of yours, neither. I hear she's a real looker.'

Clayton made the mistake of glancing up into the dark foliage to try to spot Oakley. There were two professional gunmen among the riders and both of them saw the opening to lengthen the odds. They drew their handguns with smooth, silent speed. Both sixshooters exploded at once and Clayton staggered backwards, two fountains of blood springing from his twice-punctured heart.

Men yelled and horses reared. The Winchesters of Oakley and Anson cracked, the muzzle flashes lighting up the trees for an instant. The top man in the group and one of the gunmen were pitched from their frightened mounts, both taking bullets in the backs of their necks. The second gunman brought up his Colt to snap a shot towards Oakley's position. But the youngster was already dropping from his perch as the gun swung towards him. He landed in a crouch and squeezed the Winchester trigger. The surprised gunman took the heavy calibre bullet under his jaw and it burrowed completely through his head to crash out at the top of his skull. His toppling body crashed into the unbalanced man beside him and the living man was hurled to the ground by the impact of the dead one.

'Not the big one!' Oakley yelled to Anson as the fallen man

screamed beneath the pumping, lashing hooves of the panicked horses.

One shod hoof crashed through his stomach while another caved in his head.

The three surviving riders continued to fire their handguns, unable to take aim as they tried to control their horses and wheel them for a run out of the trees. Oakley and Anson, their positions stable, had only to dodge the wildly fired bullets as they took aim. Both farmers elected a single target and a fourth Ryan man died. His right kneecap was smashed and he was crushed beneath the dead weight of his own horse, brought down by a bullet meant for the man but finding the animal.

Thus, it was only two horsemen who broke from the trees and made the open trail cutting down the brush-cloaked slope. It was a bad move, but one which frightened men could be expected to take. South lay the cover of trees, but with no guarantee there were not more armed homesteaders waiting in reserve. To the north, the country was open but there would be other Ryan men in that direction.

Edge remained crouched in the brush, but with the stock of the Winchester nestling against his shoulder. As the two horsemen galloped out of the timber, both were firmly in control of their mounts: and both were half-turned in their saddles to blast shots back towards their ambushers. The giant was a little behind the more slightly-built survivor. But he was on the same side of the trail as Edge. The half-breed tracked the target with the Winchester and squeezed the trigger when the range was reduced to little more than a dozen feet.

The giant gave a roar of rage and horror. Not pain, for he had not taken the bullet. It was his horse that tumbled, forelegs collapsing first as the lead, plunging into the wide eye, found the brain. Crimson flecked with fragments of lighter colours streamed out of the mutilated socket and splashed across the face of the giant as the man was pitched from his saddle. Because of the forward cant of the carcase, the rider was hurled across the neck and head of the animal. He crashed against the back legs of the other horse before thudding to the ground as his own mount rolled into an inert heap behind him.

The lone rider snapped his head around to stare at the tall figure of Edge straightening from the brush.

'How many more!' he yelled in panic, bringing his Colt

around to cover a new target.

'Just you, feller,' Edge muttered as he squeezed the Winchester trigger.

Two other rifles cracked a moment later. The half-breed's bullet smacked into the man's back and stretched him high, to stand in his stirrups. The shots from Oakley and Anson hit the screaming man lower down – shattering his spine. The scream was curtailed and the dead man fell to the side. One of his booted feet was trapped in the stirrup and he was dragged, upside-down, along the trail like a large hank of limp fabric – red fabric, disintegrating to leave coloured threads and larger remnants of the same hue on the bleached dirt. He was dragged a full hundred yards before his foot worked free. And his mount became just one more riderless horse to make for the peace and refreshment of the stream bank.

'Jack Clayton's dead!' the shrill-voiced Anson yelled in horror.

'Only one answer to that,' the half-breed growled against the diminishing sound of hoofbeats. He stepped out on to the trail and rested the still warm muzzle of his Winchester against the pulsing throat of the groaning giant.

'What's that, Edge?' Oakley asked.

'Bury him,' was the flat reply.

The giant, who prabably weighed more than two hundred and fifty pounds, hardly had the strength to speak. The heavy fall had knocked the wind out of him and he had cracked the side of his head against the hard-packed dirt of the trail. His face, sheened by sweat and the blood of his horse, was contorted by a grimace of pain. His gun had been hurled from his hand as he was thrown from the dead horse. He carried no other weapons in sight.

'What you gonna do, mister?' he gasped as Edge dropped down into a crouch beside him, drawing the Colt and jabbing the muzzle into the man's expansive belly.

'Be obliged if you'd let me ask the questions, feller,' the half-breed said softly, tossing the Winchester into the brush. As he withdrew his hand, it streaked to the back of his neck and he slid the razor from the pouch.

The giant vented a groan of terror as he saw the moonlight glint on the blade. And then he tried to press himself harder against the ground as the cold steel was laid across the sweat-tacky flesh of his right cheek. The end quarter inch of the blade was immediately in front of his eye.

'That's Clint Mulberry,' Anson said as he and Oakley came to stand on either side of Edge and his prisoner, rifles canted across the front of their bodies.

'He one of them who beat you up, Edge?' Oakley asked.

The giant sucked in a deep breath and spoke fast. 'Look, it was Mr Ryan's orders. I just do what I'm told.'

'Ryan runs a tight ranch,' Edge muttered. 'I guess if you heard him say shit you'd squat and strain?'

'Please, mister!' the giant groaned. 'Do what you gotta do.'

He had screwed closed the eye beneath the razor. The other one was swivelled to its fullest extent to stare at the half-breed's fisted hand.

'Who took my money, feller?'

The opened eye blinked and peered up at the impassive, bruised and cut face of his questioner. 'Money?'

'Had three grand in my saddlebag before you and your buddies started using me as a punching bag. Wasn't there after.'

'I don't know nothin' about no money, I swear it!' Mulberry replied quickly.

Edge pressed the gun harder against the big belly and exerted pressure on the flat of the blade resting on the man's cheek. 'Who's horse did I get, feller? Who put my saddle and gear on him?'

'Lincoln!' the man said quickly. 'Mr Ryan told George Lincoln to give you his gelding. Lincoln saddled him with your stuff and tied you on. I didn't see him take no money and he didn't say nothin' – '

'But he could have, uh?'

'What, mister?'

'Took the money without you or anyone else seeing him?'

The man gulped. 'Yeah, Yeah, I guess Lincoln could have done that. But he didn't say nothin' about – '

'Wouldn't have, would he?' Edge asked evenly, and lifted the flat of the blade off the man's cheek. His grip around the handle remained firm as the giant let out his breath in a sigh of relief.

'You gonna . . . ' Anson started to say. The razor plunged downwards. ' . . . let him go,' the farmer finished lamely.

The blade bit in through the lid and sliced into the eyeball.

Mulberry's scream was incredibly high and thin to be vented by such a big man. But it was short-lived. And his hands never came near to reaching Edge's fist around the razor handle. For the point of the blade went under the front of the skull and penetrated deep into the brain. The man became abruptly silent and twitched just once as his reaching hands fell back to the ground.

'God, that was awful!' Anson groaned as Edge wiped the bloody blade on the corpse's vest before he straightened and slid the razor back into the pouch.

'It was sure more than an eye for an eye,' Oakley muttered.

'I figured you were fixin' to lam into him the way he did you,' Anson said as the half-breed retrieved his Winchester from the brush.

'You hear him complain?' Edge asked.

'He didn't have no time for that,' Oakley accused.

Edge nodded as he canted the rifle to his shoulder and moved up the final few yards to enter the timber at the top of the slope. 'So Mulberry's likely thanking me right now for making it quick,' he answered. 'I never was one for beating about the bush.'

Chapter Nine

EDGE rode out on the trail alone, but by the time his gelding had drank his fill at the clear stream, Oakley and Anson were mounted and heading down the slope.

'No tools to do a proper job,' Oakley said. 'So we just covered him with fallen leaves.'

'For the best, I reckon,' Anson said. 'When it's over, I guess Marilla'd prefer to have Jack buried proper in a cemetery or on their place.'

'Be a lot of other widows burying their menfolk if you don't learn by what happened up there,' the half-breed put in as he urged the gelding to ford the stream and the two farmers trailed him.

'There's only us,' Anson said.

'Forget it, Mr Anson,' Oakley growled. 'Edge knows the plan.' The youngster moved up on one side of the half-breed and Anson took the other flank when the three horses reached dry land again. 'We should have done like you, uh?'

'Hid until the odds were evened up?' Anson said, and his shrillness had a tone of whining complaint now.

'Feller, you really are figurin' to wind up dead tonight, ain't you?' Edge asked.

He didn't have to make a move towards drawing a weapon to terrify the moon-faced farmer. All he had to do was turn to look at the man and tip his hat on to the back of his head, removing moon shadow from the wreckage of his face. Even with unblemished features, Edge could petrify lesser men

by a display of tacit, ice-cold anger. But now, the white teeth
and glittering blue slits of his eyes were given a harsher aspect
by the discoloured bruises and crustings of congealed blood on
the old cuts which distorted the taut skin stretched over the
lean features. And a near thirty-six hour growth of bristles
added to the ogre-like appearance of the face.

'Gee!' Anson gasped. 'Okay. I was wrong. I admit it. I
apolog – '

'Mr Edge means we oughta to have fired first and asked questions after,' Oakley cut in to rescue Anson from his discomfiture.

The half-breed faced front again and reset his hat squarely
on his head. 'If you've got a mind to ask any questions,' he
supplemented. 'If you ain't, it's best you don't leave anyone
alive – to answer anybody else's questions.'

'We learned the lesson,' Oakley growled. 'Shame is Jack
Clayton ain't alive for it to do him some good.'

'It was his idea,' Anson said. 'To try to take them guys
prisoner.'

'Makes you kinda like doctors,' Edge said evenly.

'How's that?' Anson wanted to know.

The half-breed's face showed wintry humour. 'You just
buried a mistake.'

He stepped up the pace to a rhythmic canter and his constant surveillance was less intent than before. The six Ryan
men had obviously met up with the surveyors, or heard about
the trouble at the Oakley homestead from somebody who had.
So it was unlikely that more men would be sent to back up the
six in taking care of such a minor incident. But alertness was
nonetheless necessary: apart from the fact that it had become
an unbreakable habit with the man called Edge.

He was a trespasser on land the rancher claimed as his own
and there could be other Ryan men out on patrol: not neces-
sarily intent upon finding Edge, but eager to blast him out of
the saddle if the opportunity presented itself.

The trio had covered some four miles from the gunfight at
the hilltop wood when Edge called another halt. The trail had
swung towards the centre of the broad valley and was running
along the western bank of the main river. They were almost out
of the primarily undeveloped section of the valley and ahead of
them the country was less convoluted. The ground was mostly

flat, with just a few slopes down towards the banks of the river. Timber grew here and there, in small clumps and large expanses of woodland. And, close to many of these stands, there were small farmhouses and outbuildings. Pasture meadows and fields of growing crops were spread around the homesteads. No light showed anywhere.

And there were no animal sounds except for the beat of hooves and snorts of the horses Edge, Oakley and Anson rode to a halt close to a house and barn.

'Kinda eerie, ain't it?' Anson muttered, his shrillness muted as he looked along and across the river. 'All these folks houses and not a sign one of them's alive.'

'Two folk ain't,' Edge said, swinging out of his saddle.

Anson and Oakley snapped their heads around to look at the half-breed. He was standing between two strips of fresh-dug earth, each about three feet wide by six feet long.

'Make a wrong move and you men'll join 'em!' a voice rasped, larded with menace.

There was the metallic clatter of repeating rifle actions being pumped. The voice and the other sounds had come from the direction of the house and barn.

'Hey, that you, Wynne?' Anson called.

'Who's that?'

Both men revealed a note of relief in their voices.

'Dale Anson and young Oakley. And a stranger in the valley name of Edge.'

There was a burst of confused talk from the homestead, then doors were flung open and two groups of men emerged. Fifteen in all, each of them carrying a rifle or revolver he was careful to keep averted from the newcomers as the group moved across the yard.

'You came then,' a rangy, red-headed man said. 'We'd about given you up. Figured you run into that bunch of Ryan hands rode past here couple of hours ago.'

Like the others, the spokesman for the group glanced only fleetingly at the two mounted farmers. Edge was the centre of attention.

'We run into 'em,' Anson said with excitement. 'Killed 'em all.' His tone became sombre. 'But they put paid to Jack Clayton.'

The group formed a half-circle at the edge of the trail and

greeted the news with a concerned shaking of heads. The half-breed splayed his legs so that each of his booted feet was atop a new grave.

'Whose?' he asked.

The spokesman continued with his responsibility. 'The two gunslingers who were guarding the city survey fellers. Their horses brung 'em here and wouldn't be spooked off. Wife made me bury 'em. Name's Zane Wynne. Mighty glad to know you.'

He extended a gnarled hand.

Edge ignored it. 'You don't know me, feller. And if you did, it wouldn't please you. You check what those fellers were carrying before you planted them?'

Wynne looked insulted by Edge's response. But he glanced at Oakley and received a tacit sign to stay calm.

'No, I didn't!' he snapped. 'They were smellin' pretty damn bad and I just got them under ground soon as I could.'

'You got the gear off their horses?'

'Yeah.'

'You check that?'

'No.'

Edge spat. 'Be obliged if you'd bring their stuff to me, feller. And I'd like the loan of a spade.'

Wynne blinked and the others shuffled their feet. 'You gonna dig 'em up, mister?'

Edge sighed. 'It might just save me the trouble of making a few other fellers fit for burying.'

'Do like the man asks, Mr Wynne,' Danny Oakley urged. 'He's lookin' for some money was stole from him.'

Wynne, who was apparently the elected leader of the group as well as its spokesman, designated a man named Curran to do the half-breed's bidding. Curran roped in another man, named Morrell, to help him. Edge took out the makings and rolled a cigarette as Oakley and Anson dismounted and swapped reports with the other valley farmers. Even after the gunmen's gear had been delivered, and fruitlessly searched, and he started to open the new graves, Edge could not avoid overhearing the talk.

Oakley gave a fully detailed account of the events at his place and Anson amplified on the gunfight with the six Ryan hands. Wynne reciprocated with the news that only two home-steaders in this section of the valley had failed to answer the call to arms. But these two had agreed to take in the wives and children of the men assembled at the Wynne place.

The whole group backed hurriedly away as Edge got three feet down into the first grave and the moist earth began to give off a sickly-sweet stench of decomposed human flesh. The half-breed covered his mouth and nostrils with a kerchief before he exposed the corpse and saw it was Royd. The gunman had died with just seven dollars and a picture of a woman in his pocket. The woman was older and heavier than Maria Oakley. But just as naked as the gunman's final view of the young Mexican bride. Edge, showing no facial reaction and making no sound of frustration, started to fill in the grave before turning his attention to that in which Doyle was buried.

'I say we ride right now!' Wynne said suddenly, his voice rising above and cutting off the rasp of low-toned conversation. 'This guy Edge has served his purpose. He got us together in a mood to fight and the first blood's been spilled.'

'Calm down, Mr Wynne!' Oakley urged, a little nervously.

'I got no objection to what the feller says,' Edge put in, not interrupting his chore of shovelling earth back into the grave. 'One thing I'd be obliged for, though.'

'What's that?' the red-headed farmer asked curtly.

'Don't bury no Ryan dead until I get there and check them over.' He showed his cold, mirthless grin as he used the back of a hand to wipe sweat from his brow. 'Doing this kinda chore gets up my nose.'

Wynne gave an emphatic nod. 'All right, mister. I guess we owe you that much.'

Edge finished filling in Royd's grave and started to open that in which Doyle was buried. 'All I'm owed is three grand,' he said as the group moved towards the barn, leaving Oakley and Anson with their horses.

'You care about anythin' else 'ceptin' money, Edge?' Oakley asked in a tone of disgust.

'It don't buy no happiness,' Anson added shrilly.

'But it makes misery a little more comfortable, feller,' the half-breed replied lightly.

The large group of men led their horses from the barn and swung up into the saddles. Most of them were in the mould of Clayton and Anson rather than Oakley. Which might be to their advantage in the fight to come, Edge mused as he continued to dig while the men streamed out northwards along the trail. It meant they had experience of living, if not fighting. And some of them might even have played a part in the War Between the States. On the Rebel side, probably, if they were Texans by birth or adoption. But Edge would not have held that against them if he had chosen to join in their war against Ryan. The war and all it meant was in the past and he had forgotten most things about it – like everything else in the past. It was only in bad dreams – and fantasies created by a pained mind in a beaten body – that memories he had elected to forget were thrust upon him.

And the memories he chose to recall? These were the hard-learned lessons on the art of survival. One such was not to get tied up with a bunch of wronged farmers hell-bent on an avenging crusade against hired guns.

The stench of Doyle emanated from the earth and he moved the final few shovelsful to uncover the putrefied corpse. Then he checked the pockets, boots and under the shirt of the dead man. In a levi pocket was a token for a Dallas cat house. In a boot were twenty one dollar bills.

'You can take it with you, feller,' he muttered, allowing the bills to flutter down like confetti on the corpse before he started to refill the grave. 'Guess the cost of being dead is about the same as living.'

Then he mounted the gelding and heeled him forward, in the wake of the eager homesteaders and about thirty minutes behind them. The group had set off at a gallop and maintained it until they rode out of sight. The half-breed held his horse to the same easy canter as before as he rode deep into the central, fertile stretch of the green valley.

The terrain far to the west and the east rose steadily to the valley's flanking ridges, but the ground he rode over stayed flat. From the signs left by the group ahead of him, he seemed to be maintaining the gap. Then, after riding around a curve of the trail that inscribed a course between two small farms, he saw that the group had enlarged. And that two wagons, heavily-laden, had joined the trek northwards.

With the wagons, the pace had dropped but Edge continued to canter the gelding, apart from when he allowed the animal to halt for water if the trail forded a stream or swerved in towards the main river again.

The early hours of the new day were well advanced and there was just a trace of grey sky behind the eastern ridges when he reached Rivertrees Bend – where three farmers had paid the ultimate price for trying to engage his help: and where he had been given the beating which was taking him back to Greenville. He saw the ashes of his campfire and the dried bloodstains left by Kelsey, Selby, Yates and himself. The three dead men had been buried close to where they died. The carcase of the horse had been heaped with earth displaced by the corpses. But the clearing up had been done before the war party reached the spot. There was no sign that the riders had halted or that the wagons had been rolled to a halt. Anger would have been fuelled on the move.

Edge saw the town of Greenville before he saw the farmers. Dawn had broken and the sun was shafting the promise of a hot day over the valley's eastern ridges. But the town on the western slope, and the floor of the valley, were still spread with the grey light of pre-sunrise. The half-breed had noticed the point at which the mounted men and their two wagons had swung off the trail to angle across uncultivated land that rose in the west. Thus, when he came in sight of Greenville and halted his horse, he knew the general direction in which to rake his eyes. And it didn't take him long to spot the concentration of men. They were waiting, in token cover, on the high ground just below the ridge above the broad shelf upon which Greenville was sited.

'You could stop a lot of people gettin' killed if you had a mind, Edge.'

The half-breed recognised the voice of Danny Oakley and he turned slowly in the saddle to watch the young homesteader lead his mare from around a miniature butte that nudged the western side of the trail.

'Nobody ever won a war without loss of life, Danny boy,' Edge replied. 'That's what it's all about – killing the enemy.'

'I mean innocent lives,' Oakley insisted as he emerged on to the trail and swung into the saddle. He eased his horse forward a few feet to halt alongside the half-breed. 'You want to know what they figure to do?'

'Not unless it puts my three grand in danger, Danny boy.'

Edge was feeling good. There was no guarantee that he would retrieve his money in town, but he had a hunch he would. This whole mess of trouble had started in the neat, clean town and it seemed fitting it should end there. His demeanour revealed nothing of his mood, but there was an easy lightness in his tone. Until Oakley delivered a response.

'Paper money, I guess?'

The half-breed had been surveying the town and the men on the high ground above it: watching the advance of brighter light down the slope as the sun inched higher.

'What's that got to do with it?' he asked as he snapped his gaze back to the freckled face of the youngster. His tone was now as sharp as the pouched razor.

Oakley was unconcerned by the change of mood: resigned to the fact that whatever was to be, was to be now that the revolt against Ryan had started. 'Ned Crosby used to mine for silver across the border. He kept a whole stack of dynamite after he took up farming.' Oakley glanced up at where the men on the high ground were now making efforts to conceal themselves. 'He's got a wagon up there loaded with six crates of the stuff. There's another wagon stacked with bales of hay. They figure to roll them both down the hill at town.'

Edge joined the younger man in peering up at the western side of the valley, which was now totally bathed in early morning sunlight. He pursed his lips. 'They can think of other things than the price of corn when they have to, can't they?'

'Just Zane Wynne,' Oakley replied. 'He's done a lot of fightin' down in South America.'

'How's he plan to get the Ryan men into town?'

'Luke Curran's been sent out to the Big R. Gonna get a message to Ryan that the valley farmers are sending a deputation to Greenville and wanna talk to him. On account of the three men that got blasted to bits at Rivertrees Bend.'

'He'll come?' Edge asked absently. 'With enough of his hands to make a hit worthwhile.'

Oakley nodded. 'We reckon so, Edge. Ryan's got the local law in his pocket and he's never wanted the state marshals in the valley. So he's always tried to talk before stirrin' up anythin' big.'

'Yeah,' Edge said, and there was still a vagueness about his side of the conversation. 'He's real anxious for folks to think he's a fair man.'

The half-breed ran exploratory fingers over his battered

face. Although aware of what high explosive could do — quite literally reduce his hopes of three thousand dollars to ashes — he could still admire Zane Wynne's plan.

'But there's no way we can get the innocent people outta Greenville!' Oakley said tightly. 'If we emptied town, Ryan and his hands would be sure to smell a rat.'

'Sure would,' Edge agreed, watching the neat little town as it came awake to greet the new day with open doors, undrawn drapes and smoke from the chimneys. 'But war don't make much of a distinction between the guilty and the innocent.'

'And it burns up money,' Oakley insisted.

Edge spat. 'Can see why you carry a Winchester, feller,' he growled.

'What?' Oakley asked in confusion.

'You and your rifle are both repeaters. And you hit the target where it hurts, Danny boy.' He showed a cold grin. 'Right in my empty pocket.'

'Then you'll do somethin' about it?' Oakley asked with controlled excitement.

The half-breed pursed his lips as he heeled the gelding forward and jerked on the reins to angle him off the trail. 'Looks like you win, feller,' he allowed.

'But you'll do it your way,' Oakley pointed out as he moved to catch up with the other rider.

'Yeah,' Edge nodded. 'Seems like old blue eyes is back in business.'

Chapter Ten

Edge stood at the second storey window of his old room in the Lone Star Saloon and watched the neatly-attired Woodrow Ryan and his foreman lead a score of Big R hands on to the main street of Greenville. Riding between the bearded, pipe-smoking rancher and the foreman with a large pad of white dressing on his cheek, was a nervous-looking Luke Curran.

But he was the only man in the bunch to be apprehensive. Woodrow Ryan, Harv London, George Lincoln, Carver, Harding and the other men Edge could not put names to all appeared confidently relaxed. For there was nothing about the town to arouse suspicion in their minds.

Only the bespectacled desk clerk down in the lobby knew of the half-breed's return to Greenville. And he had been warned into silence on the threat of a more disfiguring razor wound than Harv London had collected. For, after convincing Zane Wynne that his plan of attack was better, Edge had approached town on foot and unseen – avoiding the street and getting into the Lone Star by a side door.

Wynne might have been hard to persuade if he had had enthusiastic support for his idea. But the rest of the farmers shared the opinion of Danny Oakley – they didn't relish killing men and women with as good reason to hate the Big R men as themselves, and had only agreed to go along with Wynne because they could think of no strategy themselves.

But, Edge thought, as he backed away from the window and let himself out of the familiar room, the red-headed Wynne could be trusted to play his part. He had listened to the half-breed's words with ill-concealed reluctance at first. But then, his experience as a mercenary soldier in Latin America had swamped the initial resentment. He was forced to allow it was a better plan than his own. And the clincher for his co-operation was the fact that he would be in command of the primary attack. The tall stranger with such a wide knowledge of military tactics would simply engage in a diversionary action.

Treading silently and with the cocked and fully loaded Winchester held across the front of his body, Edge moved along the landing to the head of the stairs. Outside, there were the sounds of the Big R men halting their horses and dismounting in front of the hotel.

'Hey, feller!' the half-breed called under cover of the noise.

Dust drifted in through the open doorway. The clerk snapped his head around. The beads of sweat on his forehead caught the sun from the window as glintingly as the lenses of his spectacles. He swayed when he saw Edge and had to hook his hands over the back of the desk to stay upright.

'Just keep remembering that face you saw when you shaved this morning, uh?'

The clerk nodded vigorously and patted his brow with a spotted kerchief.

'They set the meetin' for here you say, Mr Curran?' Woodrow Ryan said as footfalls hit the stoop outside.

'That's right, sir,' the farmer answered nervously as the half-breed backed away from the head of the stairs.

There was no fear of anybody surprising him from the second floor of the hotel for he was the only guest. The only members of the staff on duty at this early hour were the desk clerk and the two bartenders in the hotel's saloon section. The bartenders didn't know Edge was back and the clerk certainly wouldn't have told them.

'Harv!' Ryan called.

'Yes, Mr Ryan?' the disfigured foreman responded at once.

'Get three or four men out on the south side of town. Up on roofs, maybe. It'll give us advanced warnin' of when our visitors come callin'.'

'You, you, you and you!' London growled. 'You heard what Mr Ryan said. Do like it.'

'Rest of you men, we'll all wait in the saloon!' the rancher announced. 'But only beer. I want everyone with clear heads in case this is some kind of trick.'

'It ain't no trick, Mr Ryan!' Curran said urgently.

'You'll be second to know if it is, sir,' the rancher answered as he entered the hotel lobby. 'Be able to tell them in hell to expect a rush.'

'It's all on the level, Mr Ryan!' Curran insisted.

'So no sweat, Mr Curran,' the rancher countered lightly. 'You and your neighbours will get a fair hearin' from me, you know that. Good morning, Ernie. Everythin' quiet?'

'Yes, sir, Mr Ryan,' the clerk responded. Too bright.

But the rancher seemed not to attach anything important to the desk clerk's attitude as he escorted Curran through into the saloon, trailed by his foreman, top hands and the other men from the Big R. Edge couldn't see them, for he stayed back from the head of the stairs until they had cleared the lobby, anxious not to be glimpsed by anybody who happened to be glancing around.

There were batswing doors at the saloon entrance on the far side of the lobby from the stairway. After they had swung closed, noise continued to come out of the saloon. Voices raised to order beer and coffee, the jingle of coinage and the scrape of chair legs against the floor. As Edge stepped forward and found himself staring down at the terrified face of the desk clerk, many conversations started, counterpointed by the clink of glasses. Cigarette, cigar and pipe smoke wafted over and under the batswings, swirling light blue in the sunlight.

Edge put a finger to his lips, then lowered his hand and jerked with the thumb. The clerk swallowed hard, nodded and ducked out of sight through a doorway behind the desk. The half-breed rested the barrel of the Winchester on the handrail, canted downwards to aim it at the saloon entrance. The noise from beyond the doorway covered the sounds of the town outside the hotel. Which was the way it would continue to be unless something went wrong. Gunshots, or even shouts of alarm, would be the signals of failure.

The clock on the wall behind the vacant desk struck the hour of eight. Edge waited. An occasional word or phrase came clear from out of the background noise in the saloon. But nothing was said to indicate the start of suspicion.

Outside, on the roofs of the Greenville City Hall and the

Valley Smithy, four men died. The weapons used against the Big R sentries were knives and lengths of baling wire. The killers were Zane Wynne, Charlie Morrell, Danny Oakley and an elderly farmer named Billy Clarke. These four men, together with a half-dozen others, had entered Greenville as stealthily as Edge while the town's earliest risers were still preparing breakfast. They had positioned themselves strategically to take care of posted look-outs for Woodrow Ryan. Only Wynne enjoyed the moment when he slid the six-inch blade of a knife into the back of his victim. The other three had to keep in mind the deaths of Jack Clayton, Selby, Kelsey and Yates in order to commit murder.

The killings were simultaneous, and took place ten minutes after Ryan and his men had entered the hotel. Edge learned of the murders when a wagon creaked into earshot. He started down the stairway then, switching his narrow-eyed attention between the saloon entrance and the hotel doorway. He was down on the floor of the lobby when the buckboard rolled to a halt outside, just beyond where the horses of the Big R men were hitched to the Lone Star rail. He recognised the leathery-skinned Ned Crosby up on the seat with the reins. Dale Anson, sweating worse than the desk clerk had been, was seated beside Crosby. Crosby, as calm as if he had been out on a Sunday hayride, glanced up and down the street and then spat between the backs of the two horse team. This was a second pre-arranged signal – that the rest of the valley farmers were closing in on Greenville for the purpose of urging the citizens to leave town.

Edge made no acknowledgement of the signal. He merely lengthened his stride, but set his feet down just as lightly, to reach the saloon doorway. He peered over the top of the doors, raking the square room in a fast glance. He saw Woodrow Ryan, sharing a table close to the bar with Curran. His men were well scattered over the smoke-layered room lounging at tables or leaning on the bar. A tight group would have been better, but the half-breed had to play the hand he was dealt.

'The boss dies first!' he snarled, opening the doors just wide enough to prod the Winchester barrel through the crack. The noise was abruptly curtailed, as if everyone had suddenly become a deaf mute. 'If anybody even blinks!'

Only eyes moved, swivelling away from Edge's head and shoulders above the doors to locate Ryan. Expressions altered from shock to expectancy. The rancher's shock was the most short-lived of all.

'My men do nothin' unless I tell them to, Mr Edge,' he said levelly, teeth clamped around his pipe.

The half-breed concentrated his attention on the bearded face. But many of the other men were on the periphery of his vision. He relied on instinct to warn him of unseen movement.

'Which one'd you tell to lift my three grand, feller?' he asked.

Ryan looked startled, and he moved. But slowly, just raising a hand to take the pipe from his mouth. 'What is that supposed to mean?' he asked. He flicked his eyes to glare at the nervous Curran. 'Are you in league with this man?' he demanded.

Curran didn't trust himself to speak. He shook his head and seemed poised to leap from his chair. But he didn't move.

'You paid me two and a half, feller,' Edge said. 'In this very hotel. And I had some travelling money when I reached town. Was in my saddlebag as far as Rivertrees Bend. After that – nix!'

The rancher was worried. He fixed Edge with a level stare. 'I gave you my word, sir. And I meant it. I would not countenance theft.'

'You got beat up for what you done to me, drifter!' London added. He was in Edge's view, standing between Harding, Carver and Lincoln at the bar behind Ryan's table. 'Weren't nothin' planned about takin' no money.'

'Best laid plans of rats and foremen,' Edge drawled, not taking his stare away from the rancher's face. 'Gonna count to ten, feller. And either somebody says something or you're finished talking for all time. One. Two. Three . . . '

Ryan looked scared for the first time since Edge had known him. 'I'll make it good, Edge!' he promised.

'Wouldn't be fair on a fair man like you,' the half-breed replied. 'All you've gained is a few seconds. Four. Five . . . '

'What'll killin' me get you?' Ryan demanded, eyes flickering to left and right like those of a cornered animal.

'Nothing,' Edge allowed. 'Which is what I've got now. So what have I got to lose, feller? Compared with you?' He sighed. 'Six. Seven . . . '

Ryan sprang erect and the move almost earned him a bullet three seconds early. But it wasn't an act of retaliation. He half-turned one way, then the other. Then glared over his shoulder.

'I'll match Edge's three grand to the man who names the culprit!' he yelled.

'Eight,' Edge said.

'Please?' Ryan begged.

'Nine.'

'Edge! I've got your money!'

The shout came from out on the street. And of those in the saloon only the half-breed and Curran recognised the voice. Danny Oakley.

Edge reacted with a narrowing of his eyes to glittering blue slits. Then: 'My mistake, feller,' he said.

He squeezed the trigger of the Winchester. Ryan and Curran dived under the bullet. George Lincoln took the lead through his heart and bounced back against the bar before crumpling. From outside came an ear-splitting explosion that rocked the Lone Star Saloon and shattered its windows. Dust billowed in through the openings. The Winchester spat two more bullets and Harding and Carver became dead weight as they completed their dives for the floor.

Then Edge was forced to retreat, whirling away from the batswings as other Big R hands drew their sixguns and blasted a hail of lead towards him. He made the foot of the stairway and glanced out through the main entrance. The buckboard with Crosby and Anson on the seat had gone. The Big R horses were still hitched to the rail, rearing and snorting in fear of the explosion and the still billowing dust.

He went up the stairway, two, three and four treads at a time. He cursed Oakley for fooling him: and himself for missing out on the second giant. He fired four shells towards the saloon, then reached the landing. He was out of sight from below when Harv London led the charge of Big R men out into the lobby. He couldn't see what happened, because he was racing along the landing. But no footfalls sounded on the stairway. Gunfire out on the street drew the men towards the main doorway. Guns exploded shots from inside the lobby, and voices were raised to give orders and counter-orders.

At the far end of the landing there was a window. It was open. Edge climbed on to the sill, but didn't go out. Instead, he reached up, and pushed open a trapdoor. Sunlight shafted in. He tossed his rifle out on the roof and climbed up after it. He snatched up the Winchester, then went out prone and bellied towards the cover of the hotel sign at the front side of the roof.

Down at the southern end of the street, the Greenville City Hall was a blazing, blackened ruin sending orange flames and oily smoke up into the morning air. And, lined up across the end of the street, mounted and with their guns holstered and booted, were the valley farmers.

'Ryan, you bastard!' Wynne yelled above the roar of flames. 'You and the Big R ain't gonna have things your way no more!'

The shout silenced the confused babble of talk in the hotel lobby for a moment. Then Ryan snarled an order.

'Go get those sodbusters! Go kill every last one of the sonsofbitches! Hundred dollars a head!'

'You heard Mr Ryan!' Harv London roared. 'Move!'

There was a burst of gunfire from the hotel entrance. The farmers wheeled their horses and lunged into galloping retreat.

'They're runnin'!' the big R foreman yelled gleefully.

There was a knot-hole in the sign. Edge put an eye to it and peered down the façade of the building as men rushed off the stoop and tore the reins from around the hitching rail. He held the rifle between his clenched knees and pushed an index finger into each ear.

Seven men swung into the stirrups simultaneously and thudded down into their saddles. Seven detonators were triggered and seven packs of dynamite sticks exploded between saddles and horseflesh. But more than seven men and seven horses died. The blast sent screaming men and panicked horses into a mêlée of collisions and more detonators were triggered.

For long moments, Edge was dazzled by the intense flare of the multiple explosion. And, even when he took his fingers out of his ears, he continued to suffer temporary deafness.

Then it began to rain debris which had been hurled high into the air. Blood-dripping, unrecognisable chunks of horsemeat and human flesh. Pieces of saddle. Twisted metal that had once been guns. Flaming remnants of clothing. Edge crouched, covering his head with his arms, until the detritus storm was over. By then his vision had cleared and he was hearing normally. He saw the returning farmers first. Then heard the beat of their horses' hooves. As he stepped back towards the front side of the hotel roof, the sign he had sheltered behind collapsed and crashed downwards. He looked after it and saw the awesome spectacle of mutilated and blackened bodies and carcases. Every man who had rushed out of the hotel to carry out Ryan's order had perished. But the mutilation of the remains was too terrible to make even a cursory count. The decapitated head of the second giant was recognisable.

Two men from the Big R had not died as a result of the exploding horses, though. Woodrow Ryan and Harv London had been inside the lobby when the chain reaction of lethal explosions began. They had been hurled back into the building by the blasts and suffered only shock and bruising. As Edge continued to look down at the result of his idea, the rancher and the foreman stepped outside, dazed but able to pick a way between the horrific remains of men and horses. Both had their hands raised above their heads.

For a moment, Edge was puzzled. But then a third man made his exit from the Lone Star Saloon. Curran, carrying a levelled Winchester. The trio moved out into the centre of the street, on the fringe of the grisly debris. The farmers slowed their horses as they approached from the south end of the street. The citizens of Greenville, on foot, shuffled forward from the north end.

It was the rancher who first sensed the half-breed's presence, and turned his shocked gaze up towards the hotel roof. His clothes and neatly trimmed grey beard were sooted and untidy now and he looked every inch a broken man.

'You're a real smart guy!' Ryan said, his voice croaky.

All other eyes swung to look at the tall half-breed atop the blackened and shattered façade of the hotel. Edge gestured with the Winchester to encompass the litter of shattered corpses.

'Real smart,' he agreed. 'Look, Ryan – no hands!'

'Went to pieces, didn't they?' Zane Wynne called happily.

'Here, Mr Edge!' Oakley yelled. 'No hard feelin's, uh?'

He stood upright in his stirrups to hurl an oil-skin wrapped package up to the roof. It arced through the acrid-smelling air and bounced on a wrenched-off hand and forearm to land against the half-breed's left boot.

'Maria don't deserve to be a widow,' Edge replied as he stooped and picked up his money. 'But if you see me again, turn and go the other way, feller.'

'Step aside, Curran,' Zane Wynne ordered, happiness gone and his face and voice heavy with menace.

'What you gonna do?' Harv London whined.

'Take it like a man!' Ryan growled.

'You're a fair man, you always say,' Wynne snarled. 'So you gotta see you should get the same as your men.'

It wasn't a part of Edge's plan, but it had been pre-arranged. As Curran stepped out of the line of fire and the citizens of Greenville backed hurriedly away, every valley homesteader save one levelled a rifle. Harv London turned and tried to run. Ryan stood rigid, swelling his chest with an intake of breath. The fusillade of rifle shots sounded somehow muted after the recent explosions. Multiple wounds were opened up in both men, and each was lifted clear of the ground before being flung down on to it. Their heads, torsoes and limbs were suddenly stained crimson by spurting blood. Scavenging flies from the blasted corpses swarmed towards fresh food.

The man who had failed to take part in the execution was the freckle-faced Oakley. He was still looking up towards Edge. Not in fear, for he had accepted the half-breed's word that he was in no danger from the canted Winchester. Edge showed a grin that held just a hint of humour.

'And Harv turned around for you, feller,' the half-breed called evenly.

Oakley blinked. 'What?'

'You could have shot him,' Edge answered. 'Kind of a swan song in this ruckus.'

'What you talkin' about, Edge?' Zane Wynne growled.

'Just seems to me,' the half-breed answered as he turned. 'That Danny boy oughta have scored a hit with the London derrière.'

THE END

EDGE: THE LONER
by George G. Gilman

First in a new Western series whose hero is the lone and sinister Edge – a new kind of Western hero, a man alone.

The idealised Westerner lives clean, is respectful to ladies, courteous to his social inferiors and gives his enemies a sporting chance.

Edge is not an idealised Westerner – not in any way at all.

Look out for Edge.

NEW ENGLISH LIBRARY

EDGE:
TEN THOUSAND
DOLLARS, AMERICAN

by George G. Gilman

Second in a new Western series, this story is set South of the Border where men live miserably and die violently.

Ten American dollars can keep a family for months. For ten thousand dollars a man would slit the throat of his own grandmother.

Edge knows where such a sum is hidden and the bandits know that he knows. The shadow of death hangs over them all.

NEW ENGLISH LIBRARY

NEL BESTSELLERS

Crime

T013 332	CLOUDS OF WITNESS	Dorothy L. Sayers	40p
T016 307	THE UNPLEASANTNESS AT THE BELLONA CLUB	Dorothy L. Sayers	40p
T021 548	GAUDY NIGHT	Dorothy L. Sayers	40p
T026 698	THE NINE TAILORS	Dorothy L. Sayers	50p
T026 671	FIVE RED HERRINGS	Dorothy L. Sayers	50p
T015 556	MURDER MUST ADVERTISE	Dorothy L. Sayers	40p

Fiction

T018 520	HATTER'S CASTLE	A. J. Cronin	75p
T013 944	CRUSADER'S TOMB	A. J. Cronin	60p
T013 936	THE JUDAS TREE	A. J. Cronin	50p
T015 386	THE NORTHERN LIGHT	A. J. Cronin	50p
T026 213	THE CITADEL	A. J. Cronin	80p
T027 112	BEYOND THIS PLACE	A. J. Cronin	60p
T016 609	KEYS OF THE KINGDOM	A. J. Cronin	50p
T027 201	THE STARS LOOK DOWN	A. J. Cronin	90p
T018 539	A SONG OF SIXPENCE	A. J. Cronin	50p
T001 288	THE TROUBLE WITH LAZY ETHEL	Ernest K. Gann	30p
T003 922	IN THE COMPANY OF EAGLES	Ernest K. Gann	30p
T023 001	WILDERNESS BOY	Stephen Harper	35p
T017 524	MAGGIE D	Adam Kennedy	60p
T022 390	A HERO OF OUR TIME	Mikhail Lermontov	45p
T025 691	SIR, YOU BASTARD	G. F. Newman	40p
T022 536	THE HARRAD EXPERIMENT	Robert H. Rimmer	50p
T022 994	THE DREAM MERCHANTS	Harold Robbins	95p
T023 303	THE PIRATE	Harold Robbins	95p
T022 968	THE CARPETBAGGERS	Harold Robbins	£1.00
T016 560	WHERE LOVE HAS GONE	Harold Robbins	75p
T023 958	THE ADVENTURERS	Harold Robbins	£1.00
T025 241	THE INHERITORS	Harold Robbins	90p
T025 276	STILETTO	Harold Robbins	50p
T025 268	NEVER LEAVE ME	Harold Robbins	50p
T025 292	NEVER LOVE A STRANGER	Harold Robbins	90p
T022 226	A STONE FOR DANNY FISHER	Harold Robbins	80p
T025 284	79 PARK AVENUE	Harold Robbins	75p
T025 187	THE BETSY	Harold Robbins	80p
T020 894	RICH MAN, POOR MAN	Irwin Shaw	90p

Historical

T022 196	KNIGHT WITH ARMOUR	Alfred Duggan	50p
T022 250	THE LADY FOR RANSOM	Alfred Duggan	50p
T015 297	COUNT BOHEMOND	Alfred Duggan	50p
T017 958	FOUNDING FATHERS	Alfred Duggan	50p
T017 753	WINTER QUARTERS	Alfred Duggan	50p
T021 297	FAMILY FAVOURITES	Alfred Duggan	50p
T022 625	LEOPARDS AND LILIES	Alfred Duggan	60p
T019 624	THE LITTLE EMPERORS	Alfred Duggan	50p
T020 126	THREE'S COMPANY	Alfred Duggan	50p
T021 300	FOX 10: BOARDERS AWAY	Adam Hardy	35p

Science Fiction

T016 900	STRANGER IN A STRANGE LAND	Robert Heinlein	75p
T020 797	STAR BEAST	Robert Heinlein	35p
T017 451	I WILL FEAR NO EVIL	Robert Heinlein	80p
T026 817	THE HEAVEN MAKERS	Frank Herbert	35p
T027 279	DUNE	Frank Herbert	90p
T022 854	DUNE MESSIAH	Frank Herbert	60p
T023 974	THE GREEN BRAIN	Frank Herbert	35p
T012 859	QUEST FOR THE FUTURE	A. E. Van Vogt	35p

T015 270	THE WEAPON MAKERS	A. E. Van Vogt	30p
T023 265	EMPIRE OF THE ATOM	A. E. Van Vogt	40p
T017 354	THE FAR-OUT WORLDS OF A. E. VAN VOGT	A. E. Van Vogt	40p

War

T027 066	COLDITZ: THE GERMAN STORY	Reinhold Eggers	50p
T009 890	THE K BOATS	Don Everett	30p
T020 854	THE GOOD SHEPHERD	C. S. Forester	35p
T012 999	P.Q. 17 – CONVOY TO HELL	Lund & Ludlam	30p
T026 299	TRAWLERS GO TO WAR	Lund & Ludlam	50p
T010 872	BLACK SATURDAY	Alexander McKee	30p
T020 495	ILLUSTRIOUS	Kenneth Poolman	40p
T018 032	ARK ROYAL	Kenneth Poolman	40p
T027 198	THE GREEN BERET	Hilary St George Saunders	50p
T027 171	THE RED BERET	Hilary St George Saunders	50p

Western

T016 994	EDGE No 1: THE LONER	George Gilman	30p
T024 040	EDGE No 2: TEN THOUSAND DOLLARS AMERICAN	George Gilman	35p
T024 075	EDGE No 3: APACHE DEATH	George Gilman	35p
T024 032	EDGE No 4: KILLER'S BREED	George Gilman	35p
T023 990	EDGE No 5: BLOOD ON SILVER	George Gilman	35p
T020 002	EDGE No 14: THE BIG GOLD	George Gilman	30p

General

T017 400	CHOPPER	Peter Cave	30p
T022 838	MAMA	Peter Cave	35p
T021 009	SEX MANNERS FOR MEN	Robert Chartham	35p
T019 403	SEX MANNERS FOR ADVANCED LOVERS	Robert Chartham	30p
T023 206	THE BOOK OF LOVE	Dr David Delvin	90p
P002 368	AN ABZ OF LOVE	Inge & Stan Hegeler	75p
P011 402	A HAPPIER SEX LIFE	Dr Sha Kokken	70p
W24 79	AN ODOUR OF SANCTITY	Frank Yerby	50p
W28 24	THE FOXES OF HARROW	Frank Yerby	50p

Mad

S006 086	MADVERTISING		40p
S006 292	MORE SNAPPY ANSWERS TO STUPID QUESTIONS		40p
S006 425	VOODOO MAD		40p
S006 293	MAD POWER		40p
S006 291	HOPPING MAD		40p

NEL P.O. BOX 11, FALMOUTH, CORNWALL.

For U.K. & Eire: customers should include to cover postage, 15p for the first book plus 5p per copy for each additional book ordered, up to a maximum charge of 50p.

For Overseas customers & B.F.P.O.: customers should include to cover postage, 20p for the first book and 10p per copy for each additional book.

Name ....

Address..

....

Title ....
(MAY)